HARD WATER
By Louise Titchener

Isbn: 9781729463345

Other Oliver Redcastle titles by Louise
Titchener:
Gunshy
Malpractice
Trouble in Tampa

Other Mystery Novels by Louise
Titchener
Mantrap
Homebody
Buried in Baltimore
Burned in Baltimore
Bumped Off in Baltimore

Other Titles
Ageless
Greenfire
Island Secrets

Since friend and foe were buried here
In one promiscuous pile —Author unknown

CHAPTER ONE

July 1884—The prow of the R.B. Hayes parted Lake Erie like a knife through silk. Oliver Redcastle stood at the rail of the steamer perusing a brochure extolling the charms of the ship's destination, Put-In-Bay, Ohio.

He read: *This delightful and salubrious island is famed for its poplar, maple, oak and eucalyptus which furnish shade to cool the fevered brow and rest the sore and weary foot and bring comfort in the eventide. In addition to the delights of the crystalline waters of Lake Erie, visitors can gratify every desire at public baths, livery and pleasure wagons, souvenir stands and general stores, etc.*

Oliver tossed the brochure into a bin and strolled toward the ship's bow. Oblivious of his passing, a pretty young woman leaned over the rail gazing pensively down at the sparkling water. He watched her covertly and considered his options. He could simply introduce himself. But such a direct approach might frighten her and ruin any further chance of getting close.

He had trailed Hermione Mussman all the way from Chicago yet hadn't found an occasion to speak to the young beauty. Indeed, this was the first time he'd seen her alone. How to seize the opportunity?

A gull skimmed his head and wheeled away into the sky. Distracted, he was checking the condition of his hat when the girl climbed over the railing.

"Don't!" He rushed at her and managed to seize a handful of her skirt. She gave him a terrified glance and then reared back. The material tore as she plummeted over the side. A woman screamed, her sharp cries mixing with those of the gulls. A gaggle of horrified passengers rushed to the rail and pointed down at the lake. The young woman thrashed silently in the foamy water, her dress billowing around her.

The R.B. Hayes's engine finally stopped, but inertia kept it moving. Already it was leaving Hermione Mussman in its wake. Oliver kicked off his boots, removed his jacket and dived in. The blow struck by the icy water almost knocked him unconscious. When he surfaced he felt as if he'd swallowed a good portion of the lake.

Half blinded, he looked for the girl. Spotting a pale blur, he stroked toward it. By the time he had closed the distance between them Miss Mussman had disappeared. Several life rings tossed by passengers floated nearby but she'd failed to grab them.

Fortunately, the water was clear. Below, Oliver made out the shape of her body and slowly flailing limbs. Diving deep, he seized her arm.

It was like pulling an anchor from a bed of clinging weeds. Kicking for dear life, he finally managed to drag her to the surface and hold her face above water. She didn't seem to be breathing and looked so pale he feared he'd been too late.

A lifeboat from the steamer rowed up. Amidst much confusion the men on the boat hauled the young woman aboard and helped Oliver out of the water.

When he'd mopped his face and cleared his vision he saw that Miss Mussman lay draped over the side of the boat. A man with a firm tone of voice was encouraging her to rid her lungs of water. When a last trickle of Lake Erie dribbled from her colorless lips he propped her against the transom and took her pulse.

She was young, no more than eighteen or nineteen. Her wet hair looked dark but would dry to a pale gold. Her sodden dress clung to her body, showing the shallow rise and fall of her high bosom and the faint curve of her belly. Her wet lashes cast dark half moons against her waxen skin.

"Will she be all right?" Oliver asked the man ministering to her.

"She swallowed a deal of lake, but now that she's breathing normally she should recover." The man assessed Oliver. "What about you? Seems you've swallowed some of Lake Erie's hard water yourself."

"I'm all right."

"More than all right, I'd say. Name's Brown, by the way."

"Oliver Redcastle." Oliver extended his hand and Brown, a handsome man somewhere in his fifties, shook it.

"You're a hero, Redcastle. I'm honored to make your acquaintance. It was mighty brave to jump in like that. You saved this young lady's life."

"Do I know you?" Oliver asked. "You look familiar."

Brown smiled wryly and shrugged. "It's possible."

Hermione opened her pale blue eyes wide and stared accusingly at Oliver. "Why? Why did you save me?" she whispered. She coughed several times, unable to say more. Finally she blurted, "Were it not for you I'd be dead now, and a much happier woman."

CHAPTER TWO

An hour later the R.B. Hayes closed in on the Bass islands. Still shivering in the sunlight, Oliver draped his folded jacket over his shoulder. His outer clothing, stained by the lake's hard water, had finally dried in the July breeze. But his socks and underwear made him feel as if he were in the unpleasant clasp of a leach. He knew for a fact that his trousers had shrunk.

Unfortunately, the change of clothing he'd packed when he'd interrupted his return to Baltimore in order to attend Allan Pinkerton's funeral had been spattered with mud on the streets of Chicago. He hadn't had time to get it cleaned. He hoped Put-In-Bay would live up to the claims in its brochure and provide him with cleaning services.

A plump young man sporting a white tam and matching flannel jacket and knickerbockers strutted up and stuck out his hand.

"Captain tells me you're the gent who rescued my fiancé, Miss Hermione Mussman. That's the young lady who accidentally fell into the water. Name's Goggins, Gabriel Goggins. I'm here to thank you."

Miss Mussman's tumble into the lake had been no accident, but Oliver said nothing of this. He shook the young man's fleshy hand and looked into his round, pink-cheeked face. His light brown eyes were as friendly and guileless as a spaniel's.

Oliver didn't need to be told who Gabriel Goggins' was. After reluctantly accepting the Mussman assignment from his former employer, William Pinkerton, he had studied a thick case file.

Doctor Leander Mussman, as the ex-actor and vaudevillian styled himself, headed a religious sect called "The Children of Paradise." He operated a mission in Toledo ministering to the poor, many of them down-and-out Civil War veterans. During nightly services held at Mussman's makeshift "Temple of Redemption" he preached that his followers could only realize their higher nature by cutting themselves off from society and submitting their wills to his divinely inspired leadership.

The cult had greatly expanded in the last four years. This was primarily owing to Leander's charismatic personality and indefatigable proselytizing. It was also due to his marriage to a wealthy spinster named Agatha Shalworth. Pinkerton's report described her as fanatically devoted to her new husband and his cause—despite the fact that he'd quickly drained her of funds.

After flattening the Shalworth bank account Leander had fished elsewhere for financial support and hooked Gabriel Goggins.

The heir of a prosperous merchant, Gabriel had become Leander Mussman's principal benefactor. Recently he'd gifted The Children of Paradise with ten thousand dollars. In return, Mussman had rewarded him with the hand of his beautiful young daughter, Hermione.

Oliver smiled at Goggins and said, "I hope Miss Mussman has recovered from her fall."

"Oh yes, praise the lord. She's resting in the captain's quarters. Her pater would be here to thank you himself, only the family is praying together."

"I see." Oliver pictured the scene. Mussman in his bombastic style would be upbraiding his daughter for her recent disobedience and demanding that she bend her will to his. The beautiful Hermione, strong-willed herself and with her own brand of showmanship judging from her flamboyant leap into Lake Erie, would be resisting in stony silence while her hatchet-faced stepmother looked on in disapproval.

Goggins continued affably, "Perhaps you know of Doctor Mussman's reputation."

"No," Oliver lied.

"He's a very holy man, a man with a bit of the divine about him."

"How is that?"

"Six years ago he had an angelic visitation. A beautiful creature appeared to him in a shower of gold and told him to go out and make the world a better place. He's doing just what she commanded."

"Oh?"

Goggins blinked his prominent eyes. "I see from your expression that you are a skeptical man. Well, I don't mind admitting I was a doubter myself. Then I got to know Leander. Changed my whole view. Take my word, if an angel were going to visit anyone it would be Leander Mussman. He's the genuine article, a truly holy man."

"How did you happen to make his acquaintance?"

"Last year my father passed, bless his poor benighted soul, and I took over his hardware business. Leander came to me seeking employment for some of his flock. He explained to me these were mostly fellas who'd been wounded in our terrible war between the states. Wounded in body, some of them. Wounded in mind and spirit—all of them."

Oliver nodded. "Unfortunately, such men are not in short supply. These United States will be knitting sad wounds for many years to come."

"Oh, indeed! I didn't have the privilege of serving in our great national conflict myself—too young, don't you know." He looked Oliver up and down. "You might have done, though."

"I did."

Goggins slapped Oliver on the back. "Thought so. There's an impression stern looking fellas like you give out—as if you've seen things others haven't. P'raps you know what I mean by 'injured in spirit'."

"I think so." Oliver knew all too well.

Goggins delivered another hearty slap. "I can always tell that about a man. You're a survivor, Mr. Redcastle. You've gone through the fires of hell and come out the other side stronger for the test."

"You flatter me."

"Your modesty speaks volumes. You're a man with a core of hardened steel. Oh, I can see that clear as day. It would take a man like that to rescue Hermione. "'Course, I would have done it myself if I'd seen what happened."

"Of course."

"Well now, Leander ministers to the fellas the war left behind, cast up on the squalid mud of this sad existence like so much worthless flotsam. He takes them in, gives their lives purpose. Once you see him at his work you become a believer. It happened to me. It'll happen to you!"

Oliver managed a silent nod, and Goggins slapped his back again. "Look here, Leander's sent me to invite you to a little banquet we're throwing for the Brethren and a few select guests. It's to be tomorrow night at the Middle Bass Club. That's a private little oasis hidden away on Middle Bass Island."

"An island close to Put In Bay?"

"No more than an hour's sail, depending on the wind. Think you might like to join us?"

"Why yes, I think I might. Thank you for the invitation."

"Capital! Be at Doller's dock at five sharp and you'll find me there with a magic carpet." Leaning close, he whispered, "This very minute as I speak to you there's a dozen of Leander's followers aboard the R.B. Hayes."

"I'd noticed a prayer circle just after we left Sandusky."

"Prayers were to bless our mission."

"Mission?"

"This is a scouting trip for the Brethren. We're looking for our own bit of paradise. Keep that under your hat for now, will you, Redcastle?"

"Certainly."

"Wouldn't want word to get out before the deal is done."

"Mum's the word."

"What about you? Headed for Put-In-Bay on business?"

"Pleasure. I've heard the Lake Erie islands are beautiful this time of year. From what I can see, that's true."

A blast from the ship's whistle cut off Gabriel's reply. The R.B. Hayes was rounding the picturesque limestone cliff that formed South Bass Island's western shore.

Rustic cottages nestled in the trees. Occasionally a cottager waved from a deck chair set up on the grass. Presently the Hayes made a turn past a smaller limestone island guarding the entrance to Put-In-Bay's harbor. As the side wheeler steamed along its rocky perimeter Oliver looked up to see what appeared to be the turret of a stone castle.

"Jay Cooke's place," Goggins volunteered. "The island is called Gibralter. Cooke owns the whole blessed place."

"Jay Cooke, the banker?"

"Truly a sainted man of business. He's the fella' who invented the bonds helped finance the Union. I expect you knew that."

"Yes."

"'Course you do. Weren't for him this land of our might still be stained with the sin of slavery."

Oliver squinted across the sunlit water. "Cooke's banking business broke up after the crash in '73, isn't that right?"

"He's had his ups and downs. Don't we all? He's rich as ever from what I hear. You'll be seeing Jay Cooke at our banquet."

The steamer nudged up against the dock, and its crew tossed lines to helpers ashore. Goggins pumped Oliver's hand again.

"I've got to get back to our party. See how Miss Mussman is doing."

"Give her my regards."

"Hope to see you at the banquet tomorrow night. Remember, Doller's dock at five."

"I'll be there."

Goggins winked. "Have the feeling this is going to be a most interesting few days for both of us, Redcastle."

"I have that feeling, too."

CHAPTER THREE

Sightseers streamed down the R.B. Hayes's gangplank and into the village of Put-In-Bay. Oliver slowed his pace to avoid a child bouncing with excitement.

Just ahead the man named Brown who'd helped pull Hermione Mussman out of the water was striding away. Hurrying to keep up with him was a more slightly built man wearing a Norfolk jacket. Staring after the pair, Oliver frowned. There was something tantalizingly familiar about Brown. He was sure they'd met before. Yet he couldn't extricate the memory tickling at the back of his skull and watched in frustration as the two men disappeared into the crowd.

Shills from Put-In-Bay's guesthouses descended on the disembarking passengers offering transportation, bargain price rooms and "home-cooked meals." Loudly flogging their wares, vendors hawking post cards, candy apples, ice and flavored waters and entertainments swarmed through the vacationers. "Blossom the diving pony!" one man wearing a sandwich board screamed. "Come see her plunge headfirst into a barrel of water!"

A boy in ragged knickers thrust a flier into Oliver's hand. Stuffing the paper into his pants pocket without looking at it, he headed across a strip of park toward the watering hole where he had been told to meet his island contact.

He entered the dark interior of a narrow storefront and scanned the crowd of drinkers. At the back of the room a short, skinny man in pantaloons held up by grimy suspenders waved at him. Oliver walked to his scarred wooden table.

"Twenty years ain't done you much hurt, Redcastle. Guess you ain't saying the same of me, eh? Take a seat and we'll talk over old times."

Oliver pulled out a chair. "Rucker?"

The man shot an uneasy look around the room. When he'd satisfied himself that nobody was listening he leaned forward and whispered, "Name's Gene Waterman now. William Pinkerton didn't tell you that."

"No."

"Allan Pinkerton's whelp always was a thoughtless S.O.B. Well now that you know I've changed my name, don't fergit. I'll explain when we're alone."

Waterman, as he wished to be called, bore little resemblance to the wiry, curly-headed young man Oliver remembered as Gene Rucker. This man's head was bald and freckled. Pads of flesh cushioned his sunken eyes. A wispy handlebar moustache and a day's growth of beard failed to hide the gaps where he was missing several teeth. Even across the table he gave off the sweetish odor of a dedicated drunk.

He said, "You look parched. Wait here and I'll fetch something to wet your whistle."

"Thanks." Oliver watched Waterman slide through the crowd around the bar. It had been more than two decades since he'd last seen the fellow. Scenes from the past flashed through his mind. When newly recruited to the Pinkerton agency, Rucker-Waterman had been boyish in appearance. He'd also been adventurous to the point of foolishness, keen to take on any job that might earn him advancement in the organization.

Something had happened during the war that had ended Rucker's employment with Pinkertons. Oliver had never known what. He had been surprised when William Pinkerton had named Eugene Rucker, nee Gene Waterman, as a contact. "Fella' needs work, and he's in the right place at the right time. Maybe he'll be useful."

Oliver had accepted that at face value. Now he wondered if there had been some other reason why William had set him up with the unappealing character that Rucker had become.

Rucker-Waterman reappeared holding two foamy mugs. He asked, "So how was the old man's funeral?"

"Well attended."

"Might have gone myself if I'd had the scratch. No such luck."

Oliver proffered a coin to pay for his drink. Waterman pocketed it and said, "Allan Pinkerton made himself a mob of enemies. I'll wager a few of those looked into the coffin to make damn sure they'd seen the last of the old devil."

Oliver shrugged. In his waning years the founder of the Pinkerton detective agency had lived behind so much security that he had been almost as much a prisoner as the many men he had helped to put behind bars.

Waterman chugged his beer and went back for another. When he returned he said, "Now that his pap's dead William's the big cheese at Pinkerton's?"

Oliver nodded.

"Heard you quit the outfit a couple of years back to start your own investigation agency in Baltimore."

"You heard right."

"Well then, how come you're here dancing to Willy Pinkerton's tune?"

"It's a long story."

"I got time."

"Two reasons. Money's good and William called in a favor."

"What favor was that?"

"Nothing that need concern you, Rucker."

"Waterman. Call me Waterman."

"All right, then. Waterman it is."

"Don't fergit again."

"I won't."

Waterman shot Oliver a resentful stare. "You always was close-mouthed, Redcastle. The one time we worked together it was like having a tea party with the sphinx. I see all these many years ain't changed that. Well, I need you to be more forthcoming. Helping you out with this deal might mean risking my hide."

"Not likely. I'll need information from you and backup. We're after a bank-robber not a murderer. I don't see much danger in store for either of us."

"Mebbe, mebbe not."

"Look here, Waterman, I'll make my situation plain. On my way back to Baltimore last week I stopped in Chicago to attend Allan's funeral. The day after his pa was laid to rest William talked me into accepting this assignment. There's a fat reward involved. Ten percent of that is yours if you help to bring it off. You want in or not?"

"How much of a reward?"

"Five thousand."

Waterman drained his mug. "We can deal better at my place. Come along. I got a rig on the other side of the park."

Waterman's rig was a weathered wood cart hauled by an ancient nag who expended most of her small store of energy flinching away the biting flies swarming around her flanks. As Oliver headed toward the cart he caught sight of a group of three gaily dressed women leaving an ice cream parlor. Though he could see only their backs, the shape of one of them made him stutter-step on the wooden sidewalk. The women disappeared around a corner leaving him squinting into empty space. No, he told himself, his eyes were deceiving him.

Louise Titchener

A few minutes later he and Waterman left the
waterfront behind. They rolled along a dusty road
lined with fields of trellised grape vines. A gentle
breeze perfumed with their musky scent sighed
through oak trees partially shading the lane. The clop
of the horse's hooves and the creak of the wagon
wheels, buzzing bees and the drowsy twitter of birds
made the only other sounds.

Sweat sheened Waterman's skin and mottled
his already none-too-clean shirt. He said, "What did
William tell you about me?"

"Only that you lived here and might be
helpful." Actually, William had said that the war had
turned Rucker/Waterman into a "good-for-nothing
loafer who'd do anything for money so long as it
didn't put his worthless hide in danger."

They swung off the larger road onto a narrow
dirt track that snaked through woods choked with
undergrowth and deadwood. Waterman swatted a
mosquito feeding on his neck. "Seems like every bug
in creation comes off this damned lake."

"So I noticed. Fair amount of poison ivy
hereabouts, too."

"Poison ivy and poison varmints. Some
human."

"What do you mean?"

"Place may look like the Garden of Eden but
bad things happen from time to time."

"Such as?"

"Oh, there are stories," he said vaguely.
"People disappear, drown, things like that. Last year a
couple of tourists up and vanished. No one can figure
what happened to 'em. Me, I think they just got drunk
and fell off the dock."

"Bodies never turned up?"

"No, but that ain't unusual. Old Lake Erie has a way of swallowing down bodies."

"Interesting."

"You're wondering how I happened to wash up on this place, ain't you?

"The thought crossed my mind."

"Sure it did. You're thinkin' only a no-account bum would live on an isolated speck of dirt like this."

"Actually, I think your island is beautiful. I can see why a man might want to retire from the world here."

Waterman curled his lip. "Don't call it my island and don't deny you've writ me off as nothing but a low-life busthead! I ain't stupid! I can tell what's going on behind them cold gray eyes of yours. Well, let me tell you another thing. There's a reason I ain't exactly in mourning for Allan Pinkerton. It was him put me in this fix."

"How's that?"

Waterman scowled. "Mebbe I'll give you the story some time and maybe I won't. For now all you need know is I'm here with my name changed to save my hide. There's people who'd skin Gene Rucker alive if they could find him. And that's Allan Pinkerton's doing."

He jerked the rains to guide the wagon onto a narrow track rutted with hackberry roots. It led to a tumbledown cabin surrounded by knee-high grass.

"Place ain't much, but it keeps the rain off." He alighted from the wagon. "Put your things inside and then we'll wet our whistles. I can tell you most anything you want to know about the island. Been holed here since '63."

Oliver walked through the cabin door and resolved to find different accommodations in the morning. He wasn't a fastidious man and over the years he'd camped in some unhygienic places. The worst of these would have been preferable to the stink of Waterman's filthy, bug-ridden abode.

The rocky ledge in front of the cabin, on the other hand, afforded a breathtaking view of Lake Erie. That evening the two men sat before a fire watching a magnificent sunset and eating wild game washed down with some of Waterman's private brew.

"I see you ain't lost your sharpshooter talent," he said, forking up a piece of the pheasant Oliver had bagged for their dinner."

"Comes in handy now and then."

"We'd been eating fish if you hadn't shot these birds. I get sick and tired of fish. Say, could you pick off that cat?" Waterman pointed at a tabby slinking low to the ground near a stand of cottonwood.

"Why should I want to murder a house pet?"

"That ain't no damned pet. It's a sneaking varmint!" Waterman grabbed Oliver's rifle but before he could raise it the animal disappeared. He threw down the gun in disgust.

Oliver stared at the spot where the cat had seemed to dissolve into thin air. "Where did it go?"

"Found hisself a hidey hold. What does it matter? I'll get him one of these days. I'll make him sorry he was ever born."

"I don't see a hole over there. I'll have a look." Oliver started to get to his feet.

Waterman restrained him. "Let it be. You're a different man if you won't even put a bullet into a cat. Way I remember, you used to be mighty quick on the trigger."

"That was then. This is now."

"What's that mean? Been tamed by a pretty little wife waiting in Baltimore?"

"No wife. I do have a daughter. She's not in Baltimore now, though."

"Where is she?"

"Out west. Chloe suffers from congested lungs. Baltimore in summer is no fit place for a child with bad lungs. I took her west to spend the summer in a more healthful environment. I was on my way back when I got word Allan died."

"Hmmm. Chloe. Pretty name. You ain't got a wife but you got a sick kid named Chloe? Who's taking care of her in Arizona?"

"How'd you know it was Arizona?"

"Guessed. Back in the old days you bagged a lot of train robbers in Arizona. You probably still got contacts there."

Reluctantly, Oliver nodded. He regretted mentioning his child to the likes of Waterman. He supposed it was because he worried about Chloe. What if something went wrong while he was far away? What if he'd made the wrong decision? He poked the fire. "Let's get back to the subject at hand, shall we."

"Suits me. Tell me where this five thousand you mentioned is coming from."

"Northwest Continental. They hired Pinkerton's to catch their thief. Pinkerton's hired me."

"Must be a hell of a thief. How much did he steal?"

"A half million in specie, bonds, jewelry and other valuables."

Waterman narrowed his eyes. "You wouldn't be chasing this train-robbing wonder they're calling 'The Black Bandit' would you?"

"That's exactly who I'm chasing. What do you know about the case?"

"Only what I read. Got himself on the roof of a hotshot carrying cash to the western banks. Broke in while the messenger was checking waybills with his back to the door. They call him the "Black Bandit" because he was dressed all in black and wore a mask. Must have the luck of the devil."

"Took more than luck for a lone man to pull off that robbery. He bored a hole in the front door of the car and sawed out a panel. Cut the brake hose at the rear of the money car with the engine traveling at full speed."

Waterman whistled.

"Squeezed through the opening he'd made and surprised an armed messenger. All this wearing a hood over his head with only the eyeholes cut out. Our man is athletic, smart, and nervy."

"Got him figured yet?"

"Pinkerton's has put a name to him. Frank Aballo. He made quite a reputation for himself robbing trains out west. Got caught and escaped his cell after serving only two weeks of a five year term."

"Slippery s.o.b."

"Very slippery. Before he took to robbing banks out west he was traveling with a circus."

"Doing what?"

"Trapeze artist."

"It would take a trapeze artist to do what you describe. What makes you think you'll find him here?"

"A pretty preacher's daughter named Hermione Mussman."

CHAPTER FOUR

The next morning Waterman guided his cart down Catawba Avenue. Next to him Oliver scratched one of several mosquito bites blossoming on his neck.

Waterman aimed a gob of spit at the road. "I warned you'd be feeding the bloodsuckers if you slept outside."

"Right."

"Suppose you preferred the ground cause you're too particular to bunk with me. You ain't changed one bit, Redcastle. Still bullheaded and talkative as a stone post. Where you want to drop off?"

"The Beebe House."

"Mighty high on the hog. You going to invite me to dinner there?"

"Not tonight. Mussman's outfit is throwing a private dinner at the Middle Bass Club, and I'm going to attend."

Waterman whistled. "Hoity-toity. You'll be rubbing elbows with tycoons. Suppose that don't include me."

"Why should it? You've never even met Leander Mussman."

"Maybe that's because I got too much pride to line up at his mission for a handout. Not like this Eyetalian fellow you're nosing after. He sweet-talked the daughter in the preacher's breadline, ain't that right?"

"Aballo showed up at The Temple of Redemption a week or two after he escaped prison, probably wanting a free meal. When he saw Hermione he got religion. He became a convert and joined her Bible study class."

Waterman leered. "I see how it went. Them two were studyin' more than the Bible. Her Daddy sniffs it out and gives Aballo the boot. Lover boy robs a train and sugars his next love letter to the Mussman girl with a diamond ring from his loot."

"The letter was intercepted by her stepmother, Agatha Shalworth Mussman. Agatha watches over the girl like a hawk. It was probably Agatha who scotched Aballo's affair with Hermione in the first place. It was certainly Agatha who turned Aballo's letter over to the authorities."

Waterman picked at his teeth. "Dim-witted of the young fool to send the girl stolen jewelry. If it weren't for that you might never have caught on to him."

"We're still a long way from catching this thief."

"That's how you'll stay if he don't come panting after the girl's skirts. Why would a wanted man with any sense risk getting cornered on an island like this?"

Oliver answered impatiently. "Because the Mussmans are here for the summer. Aballo is a daredevil and men in love don't always think straight."

"Ain't that the truth. I got to get myself a look at this female, see if she's worth the fuss. How pretty is she?"

"Pretty enough. Pinkerton's is betting Aballo will follow her, maybe even try to run off with her. If he does it's your job to let me know he's on the island and my job to catch him. Are there places around here where a wanted man could hide?"

Waterman scratched his ear. "There's the woods. There's caves."

"The island has caves?"

"It's a regular old Swiss cheese."

"What about the other islands in the area?"

"Wouldn't take much of a swimmer to make it to Gibralter, or even to Middle Bass. That's where you'll be going tonight for your banquet. A rowboat would get a man to Ballast or Sugar or North Bass. Then, of course, there's Gull. Hear tell that's the island Mussman wants to buy."

"He's looking to establish his religious community there."

"So they say. You couldn't make me live on Gull Island. Place is nothing but bird shit and snakes."

"But it's close by?"

"Close enough I guess. What's this Aballo look like?"

Oliver fished a circular out of his jacket pocket. It showed a handsome young man in circus tights. A handlebar moustache disguised the lower half of his face.

Waterman glanced at the image. "That don't help. Man's not likely to be walking around in such a foolish outfit. By now he's probably shaved off the face hair. Don't suppose he speaks with a Eyetalian accent?"

"His parents were immigrants but he was born in Cinncinnati. We're looking for a fit young man, average height, brown hair."

"That describes half the young bucks vacationing on Put-In-Bay, not to mention all the summer help. You're looking for a needle in a haystack."

"Maybe, but only one man is wanted by the law and scheming to run off with Hermione Mussman. Find out if a man meeting his description is acting suspicious and keep your ear to the ground."

Waterman's rig pulled up in front of the Beebe, a large hotel skirted with handsome verandas. Oliver bid Waterman goodbye and climbed out of his rickety wagon.

A few minutes later he dropped his valise on the floor of his hotel room and stood at the window scanning the view of Put-In-Bay's harbor humming with fishing boats, pleasure craft, and steamers coming and going from Cleveland, Toledo, Sandusky and Detroit.

The scene made him think of Baltimore. Yet this northern island felt profoundly different from the city where he'd recently made his home. Baltimore's waterfront teemed with every race and nationality and welcomed commerce from every corner of the globe.

The faces Oliver saw around Put-In-Bay's Midwestern lakefront were mostly white. The water was fresh. No crabs, oysters or jellyfish lurked in its depths. On the other hand, a criminal might well be lurking in one of the island's caves. He hoped so. He wanted to catch Frank Aballo, repay his debt to William Pinkerton and go home. But what would he find at home? Only an empty house and a pile of bills, he reminded himself. With Chloe and his housekeeper, Mrs. Milawney, away in Arizona, there really wasn't much to go home to.

His gaze wandered to a small desk supplied with ink and paper. On impulse he pulled out the chair in front of it and began a letter.

Dear Chloe, I hope that you and Mrs. Milawney are settled by now and enjoying the clean, dry Arizona air. How do you like living on a ranch? I wish I could have stayed there with you. Perhaps I can join you later in the summer. I could teach you to ride a horse.

He read through what he had written and frowned. It sounded so stiff and formal, not at all what he intended. Almost two years since Chloe had come into his life. Yet he was still awkward with her. He wanted to tell his daughter that he missed her and worried about her. Why was it so difficult to put what he really meant into words that an eight-year-old child would understand?

He sighed. They had started their life together badly. When Chloe's mother, a feckless actress named Marietta Dumont, had supposedly died of Influenza, her servant had brought the child to his hotel room in Chicago. Up until that moment he hadn't even been aware that he had a daughter. Naturally the little girl had been frightened at being dumped on a strange man in a strange city. She had wept buckets and begged for her mother.

In his ignorance and confusion he had not known how to help her adjust. But he had accepted her as his own and done his best to make a home for her. He had quit his wandering life as a Pinkerton detective and set up what he hoped was a stable domicile in Baltimore. Now, two years later, he prayed they were past the worst of their early trouble. Still, though Chloe called him Papa and no longer feared him, the distance between them remained. Oliver crumpled his half-written letter. He would try again later.

After he unpacked and took stock of his wrinkled shirts and unsatisfactory supply of underwear he went to the washstand and poured water from the ewer into the basin. He noticed a reddish stain on the china and wondered about the quality of the water. Droplets had splashed around the washstand and left residue. Even the towels, when he wiped his wet hands, showed faint streaks of reddish brown—almost as if he'd been dabbing at blood. Was such hard water safe to drink?

He wanted a shave and a freshly laundered shirt. The night spent at Waterman's had done nothing to make him feel refreshed. Just before dawn he'd climbed down to a rocky beach and bathed in the lake. But he'd had to dress himself in his old clothes, shrunken and discolored from his plunge in Lake Erie the previous day. Hoping to refurbish his meager wardrobe, he set off to discover what the village had to offer.

Several shops fronting the park stocked apparel calculated to appeal to the holiday-crowds off the steamers. Oliver purchased a pair of white flannel trousers with a matching box jacket, a blue and white striped soft-collared shirt and a straw boater. Feeling slightly ridiculous in this outfit, very different from his usual rather somber apparel, he bundled up his soiled clothing and sought out the laundress the hotel clerk had recommended.

He had just left the main street for a dirt road when he heard a strident voice coming from a patch of weedy ground behind a storefront.

"Ladies and gents, this awesome equine is no ordinary horse. Blossom is a diving wonder! A four-legged hay-eating acrobat! For the paltry sum of a nickel she'll amaze and astonish you!"

Two dozen or so people were gathered around a skinny old man with a top hat, white beard and cutaway coat. "Professor Paradise and the Diving Marvel," a red and white sign in front of a makeshift podium proclaimed.

At the "professor's" loud urging, the crowd threw coins into his hat and then cheered while he led an obviously reluctant pony up a makeshift ramp. Positioned ten feet below the ramp was a shallow tub of water. A few minutes later the unhappy animal had plunged into the tub and somehow emerged dejected but unscathed. Feeling sorry for the pitiful beast, Oliver shook his head and turned away.

A ten-minute stroll from this sorry spectacle he stopped at a small wooden cottage with a sign in the window advertising cleaning services and a room to let. He was about to stroll up the gravel path to the front door when two women appeared around the side of the house. He recognized Agatha and Hermione Mussman.

Hermione's tight-waisted dress showed off her fine figure. Sunlight drew fire from the golden ringlets arranged around her creamy neck. Oliver could see why a hot-blooded young man might risk capture for such a beautiful girl.

He tipped his boater. "Miss Mussman, I believe."

She paused, stumbling slightly. Despite the shadow cast by her parasol, he detected a flush creeping across her cheek."

Her stepmother, a sparrow-like woman with a sharp nose and sharper expression snapped, "Sir, what is the nature of your acquaintance with this young lady?"

Miss Mussman tugged at her step mother's black leg-o'-mutton sleeve. "Please Agatha, it's all right. This gentleman rescued me when I fell into the lake yesterday. I haven't had the opportunity to thank him." To Oliver she said, "Please accept my gratitude, sir."

Agatha Shalworth Mussman slitted her eyes. "So you're the man who jumped off the boat. Brave of you. The water must have been cold."

"Only slightly cold. I hope Miss Mussman received no injury and has recovered from her ordeal."

"Oh yes," the girl declared, "I'm fine. Thank you." And with that, the two ladies hurried away.

Oliver stared after them. Would he be seeing Hermione at tonight's banquet, he wondered. If he did, how could he have a private conversation with her? Though still closely chaperoned by the ever-present Agatha, she looked considerably more cheerful than she had yesterday when she had been suicidal. Why, he asked himself. Had she heard from her lover? Could Aballo be on the island already?

A tow-haired boy of about ten ran around the side of the cottage. He slid to a stop and pointed at the bundle under Oliver's arm.

"You come to have washing done?"

"If Mrs. Stojack lives here. I was told she does laundry."

"I'm Billy Stojack. Mama's around back. You a day-tripper? Takes time to wash and dry laundry."

"I plan to stay on the island for several days."

"Then maybe you'd like to have me show you around. Nobody knows Put-In-Bay better than me. I won't charge much. I'm good at running errands, too. You need an errand boy just say the word."

Oliver thanked the enterprising Billy and followed him around the back of his house where Mrs. Stojack, a short, plump woman with an untidy bun of blond hair streaked with gray, toiled at washtubs set up at the rear of her cottage.

A half-dozen fair-haired children, obviously Billy's younger siblings, stirred suds with huge wooden paddles, operated a hand ringer and stood on wooden stools draping wet clothing onto a network of heavily laden lines.

When Oliver asked Mrs. Stojack about her services she straightened her damp apron and said briskly, "I charge a nickel a piece for ironing. Unmentionables washed clean and dried wrinkled are a penny. That may seem dear to you but it's not easy to keep clothes clean on this island. Water's so hard I have to use extra bleach to deal with the stains."

Remembering the reddish stains he'd seen on his wash basin, Oliver nodded his sympathy. "Your prices sound reasonable to me. What about this suit?" He shook out the bundled clothing he'd worn to Allan Pinkerton's funeral."

Mrs. Stojack cocked her head. "That's muddy wool. Best I can do is brush away the dirt and iron out the creases."

"Then that will have to do. Will it be ready by this evening?"

She pointed at a hill of colorful outfits. "Not likely, not when I have that great heap to see to!"

Oliver looked more closely at the motley pile. "Those look like theatrical costumes."

"That's exactly what they are. And you've no idea how dirty and ragged they were when they came in. Mending and washing all day I've been. You can see I'm nowhere near finished. Look at that lace," she said, poking at a frayed bit of trimming. "I'll never get it clean, not with the hard water we've got here. And if I use too much bleach it will fall to pieces."

"Is there a theatrical troupe on the island?"

"So they call themselves. To me they look more like a bunch of gypsies. Camped out on Peach Point, they are and planning to put on a play every night this week."

"Really? What sort of play?"

Mrs. Stojack had turned out the pockets on Oliver's jacket. "Here," she said, "pulling out a crumpled paper. "Why ask me when this tells you all about it?"

Oliver took the paper from her and smoothed it. Vaguely he remembered an urchin thrusting the sheet into his hand the day before. In fact, now that he thought about it, the urchin had probably been Billy Stojack. He read the bold script printed at the top.

"The Elysian Players proudly proclaim William Shakespeare's most beloved comedy, A Midsummer Night's Dream, is to be performed amidst the shady bowers of Lake Erie's most enchanted isle."

His eye ran down the page and froze. "Starring as the fairy queen Titania, fresh from triumphs on all the stages of Europe, the beautiful Miss Marietta Dumont."

Oliver squashed the paper in his fist.

CHAPTER FIVE

That afternoon Oliver stopped in front of the aptly named Round House Café. Situated on the main street and looking out at the park, it was, in fact, a round wooden structure with a domed roof. The shady interior provided a welcome relief from the July sun.

A noisy family party enjoying ice cream and phosphates crowded a table in the corner. Oliver selected a table at the back and ordered a plate of fried perch, a Lake Erie delicacy that had been recommended to him at the village barbershop.

After leaving Mrs. Stojack he'd treated himself to a shave and haircut. Feeling better for being freshly groomed, he dug into his food and considered the gossip he'd overheard amongst the men waiting their turn for a trim.

On a map of the upper Midwest South Bass and its sister islands were tiny dots in the southwest corner of Lake Erie. Yet the islands hosted a surprising number of rich and prominent men.

One of the barber's patrons had talked of the newly formed Western Canoe Association. The club attracted wealthy Midwestern sportsmen holding their annual meet on a privately owned island named Ballast.

Oliver had noticed several graceful sailing canoes in Put-In-Bay's busy harbor. With their canvas bellied in the wind they were a beautiful sight, hardly what he thought of as canoes at all. Trimmed in nickel and silver plating and decked with flags and pennons they were rich men's toys.

The barbershop gossip had mentioned the name of Ballast's principal owner, George W.Gardner, a business partner of John D. Rockefeller's. Oliver had worked for Rockefeller. The millionaire tycoon seemed to have connections to everything and everyone. He was like an austere spider sitting at the center of a web that spread its sticky net across the entire country.

As Oliver contemplated this disturbing image a shadow fell over his plate. The fragrance of lavender mingled with the smell of fried fish. His stomach gave a lurch, and he turned his head.

"Hello Ollie. Enjoying life on the island?"

"Marietta."

She walked around the table and pulled out a chair. "You don't mind if I sit down, do you?"

Forewarned by Mrs. Stojack, Oliver was able to maintain a neutral expression-even though he felt as if he'd been kicked in the stomach. He shrugged.

Marietta was not the dewy young goddess she'd been when they'd first met, but she was no less beautiful. The cynical glint in her green eyes was harder than he remembered and faint lines creased the corners of her full lips. But her red hair was as lustrous as ever, curling around her milky forehead and throat like living fire. A pale green bonnet framed her lovely face. A matching muslin gown with a low neckline emphasized the perfection of her dazzling bosom.

With a careless gesture, she untied her bonnet strings and tossed the hat on the table. "You don't seem surprised to see me."

"I'm speechless."

"That would hardly be a new development. You never were much of a conversationalist. Of course, when we were together we really didn't do much talking, did we?" She smiled seductively.

"What do you want?"

"Why, to renew our acquaintance. What else? Did you know I was on the island?"

"I saw a playbill this morning."

"And you didn't seek me out immediately?" She pretended to pout. "I'm hurt."

"Stop playing games! Why the devil aren't you in England?"

She laughed. "I wondered how long before you asked, and it wasn't long at all. Come now, Ollie, did you really think you'd got rid of me for good?"

"That was the bargain. I beggar myself to pay for your luxury cruise to England and you remove yourself from my life."

"You mean, of course, that you expected me to remove myself from our daughter's life. How very unnatural. I am her mother."

Oliver felt his jaw tighten. "Speaking of unnatural, you gave up your right to call yourself her mother when you lied, when you pretended to be dead and abandoned her. Chloe is my daughter now and mine alone."

Marietta averted her eyes. Her mouth quivered. For a moment Oliver thought she might cry. He told himself she had always been a convincing actress. Days before she'd left him for a richer man she'd made him believe she was madly in love with him and him alone. That had been nothing but sham. He hardened his heart.

When Marietta looked at him her eyes were dry. "I had no choice but to send Chloe to you. My protector had left me. I had no money, no way of caring for her."

"Why instruct your maid to make up that cock and bull story that you were dead?"

"I wasn't sure you'd take Chloe if you believed I was alive."

"You could have come to me with the truth."

"I wish I'd known that, Ollie. After the way I left you I thought you'd never take me back. I wasn't even sure you'd believe that Chloe was yours."

"Is she?"

"Yes, but I can't pretend I didn't have another lover."

Her words flicked a raw place. He said, "It doesn't matter how Chloe came into this world. She's my daughter now, and I intend to protect her."

"From what? From me? You can't honestly believe she needs protection from her own mother."

"I can when her mother is a heartless piece of goods. When you showed up in Baltimore last year you claimed you wanted to be re-united with Chloe. It wasn't true. You wanted to use her to blackmail me for passage to England. Well, you succeeded. I gave you money in exchange for your promise to disappear. I kept my word. It's time you kept yours!"

Marietta flinched. "How can you say such a cruel things to me? I was never heartless, only young and misguided. You can have no idea what it's like to be a woman utterly alone and desperate to make a place in the world. When I came to you in Baltimore I did want to see Chloe. I only agreed to take your money because I thought it might be my last chance to get back on my feet."

"Did you get back on your feet?"

She sighed. "Not in England. Oh I tried hard. I think I auditioned in every theater and music hall in London. My style was not to their taste. I failed in Europe and had to come back home. I was lucky to scrape together the money to book my return passage in steerage."

"You went first class at my expense."

"True enough, but the voyage home was quite a different matter. It was not pleasant."

"I can imagine."

"No, you're a man so I really don't think you can imagine. But it turned out well. In New York I met an old friend touring with The Elysian Players. She introduced me to the manager. I joined the company, and I'm doing well enough."

"Good."

"You say that with such disapproval in those cold eyes. Listen to me, Ollie. I'm not the foolish girl I was. I'm older now, and I've changed."

"We're both older and wiser, Marietta. I made a damn fool of myself over you once. I'll not do it again."

She glared and flattened both of her hands on the table. "I needn't ask your permission to see my own daughter. I could just go to Baltimore and meet her. I should have done that in the first place."

"You would be wasting your time and the price of a train ticket. Chloe's not in Baltimore."

"What?" She looked shocked. "Where have you hidden her?"

"Some place safe, a place that's good for her health."

"You're lying."

"I don't lie. You know that."

Marietta seized his hand. "Please, let me see her! Let me hold my baby in my arms."

Tearing himself from her grasp, Oliver slapped money on the table to pay for his lunch. He and Marietta had caught the attention of several Round House patrons. Ignoring their curious stares, he marched out of the café and hurried toward his hotel.

He glanced over his shoulder to make sure she hadn't followed. The street was empty. Looking blindly ahead he increased his pace. Preoccupied by the acid mix of emotions churning in his belly he stumbled over Billy Stojack.

"Didn't you hear me calling your name?" the towheaded youngster demanded after he righted himself.

"No, sorry."

"I been running after you ever since you left the Round House."

Oliver fished in his pocket for a coin. Billy's small, dirty hand closed around it. "My ma told me to tell you your suit's all cleaned up. You can get it any time you want."

CHAPTER SIX

Later that afternoon Oliver donned the frockcoat and trousers Mrs. Stojak had brushed into respectability and studied his image in the mirror.

He saw a tall, lean man with flecks of silver at his temples and deeply carved lines from nose to mouth. If Marietta had aged since they'd been lovers, he had aged more. Did the woman have any idea how he'd suffered over her? He hoped not.

He sat down at the desk and re-read his letter to Chloe. He had worked on it for the last hour but conceded to himself that it wasn't much different from the unsatisfactory note he'd torn up earlier. The only substantial difference was that it would be accompanied by a gift he'd selected at a shop in the village--an expensive glass ball depicting the main street of Put-In-Bay in winter. He shook it and watched snow whirl and then fall over the tiny enclosed world.

There was something appealing about the scene, so perfectly benign, so sealed from outside threats. He hoped Chloe would like it and that it would serve better than his stiff letter to say that he was thinking of her.

After mailing the letter and boxed up gift he walked to the harbor to keep his appointment with Gabriel Goggins. On the way he spied Professor Paradise leading "The Diving Marvel" out of town. At least the poor animal would get a bit of rest before facing another perilous day leaping into a shallow pool.

Oliver stepped onto Doller's dock. The summer sun, still high in the cloudless sky, sparkled over a multitude of fishing and pleasure craft bobbing at their moorings.

Directly across from the dock the dark green hump of Gibralter island squatted like a dozing porcupine. White birds sprinkled its rocky beach. Beyond Gibralter, Middle Bass could be seen. In the distance Ballast island floated pale green in the late afternoon haze.

A canoe with a half-furled sail skimmed up to the dock. Gabriel Goggins guided it, one of his arms draped over the tiller while his other hand held a line attached to the flapping sail.

"Ho there, Redcastle! Ready for a ripping good evening?"

"Looking forward to it."

Buttoned into a morning coat and long tight pantaloons, Goggins seemed an incongruous boater. The heavy links of a gold watch chain glinted against his well-padded double-breasted silk waistcoat. A large diamond stickpin adorned his neckcloth. He lounged on an oriental rug spread along the floor of his handsome vessel. He said, "I wondered if you'd show up."

"Why wouldn't I? Only a fool would miss a banquet."

"Well said! Anyone can see you ain't no fool." He laughed heartily at his own witticism. "Well, I say the gent who saved Miss Mussman deserves a swell feed." He jabbed a finger in the direction of Middle Bass. "We'll both get that on yonder enchanted isle."

"Are we going in this boat?" The canoe banged incessantly against the dock's wooden pilings, sending up little plumes of water that slopped over its gunwales. Oliver had expected to be transported in something more substantial.

"Course! Why not? She's named Magic Carpet. An apt appellation, if I say so myself. Hop in."

This was not so easy. Somehow Oliver managed to drop into the unstable canoe without tipping it over. When he was safely crouched in front of its tall mast Gabriel pushed off.

Once Magic Carpet had maneuvered through the busy harbor and past Gibralter's wind shield, a pleasant Southwesterly breeze sent it skimming across the lake. Exhilarating though the sensation was Oliver would have found it pleasanter if his feet hadn't been wet from water puddled on the boat's floor. The oriental rug was wet.

"We'll be there in a jiffy," Gabriel shouted as he adjusted a line.

"I hadn't realized you were a sailing man."

"Oh yes, been racing all my life. Didn't get into sailing canoes until a couple of years back. Best sport in the world!"

"You're a member of the American Canoe Association?"

"Indeed I am! Finest outfit around!"

Goggins explained that he was an active participant in the newly formed Association's annual race week. This being the case, he wasn't lodging at The Beebe with the Mussman party. He was camped on Ballast Island with the other well-heeled club members, many of whom he had persuaded to attend the Mussman banquet in hopes they would contribute to the preacher's cause.

"Some of the most influential men in the Midwest belong to the ACA, if I do say so myself. Good eggs, most of them. Bound to see the merit of Leander's project."

"You mean his campaign to buy Gull island?"

"Why, sure. Think what that saintly man could do with an island of his own."

"Just what are his intentions?"

"Why, to set up a community where order and sanctity prevail, a refuge for the poor and downtrodden." Goggins round cheeks grew pink with emotion. He exclaimed, "Such a paradise of goodness and virtue would serve as an example to all the world. And we'd have it right here among us on our own Lake Erie."

"Admirable, perhaps, but why would rich men who enjoy recreation on these islands want to help make them into a refuge for the poor?"

"Look here, Redcastle, you're thinking negative. You suppose that bankers and businessman won't want to part with their cash to help a fella who's down and out. Oh, some are like that, I grant. But not all. Not me, for example. I've always been willing to lend a hand where it's needed. Noblesse oblige, don't you know. It'll be my job to help the fellas who come tonight to see the right way of thinking." Gabriel winked. "I can be pretty persuasive."

"I'm sure you can."

"That's all due to Leander. He taught me how to think positive."

"He must think the world of you."

"Enough of me to let me have his daughter's hand in marriage. I guess that's pretty high praise."

"I should say so. But then, you've done a lot to earn it."

"Oh no. It's they, the Mussmans, who've done everything for me."

"How's that?"

"Until Leander came into my life I had money but nothing else, not what counts anyhow." He thumped the spot over his heart. "To be honest, I was a bit of a loose cannon. Papa had died and left me everything. But I had no interest in his business. I didn't know what to do with myself. Meeting Leander changed all that."

"In what way?"

Gabriel shot Oliver a shy, almost shamed look. "Always been a bit of an outsider. Never felt that I quite fit in. Leander changed that. He gave me a place where I could belong. Gave me a purpose. Now I don't feel alone in the world. It bucks me up to know that I've a job to do, a job that's really important."

Suddenly Oliver thought he understood Gabriel. Behind his hale-fellow-well-met bravado he was a chubby boy unsure of himself. Leander Mussman had provided Goggins with a sense of place that gave him the confidence he'd lacked. He had also provided him with a beautiful fiancé. Was Goggins totally ignorant that the beauteous Hermione was in love with another man?

Answering Oliver's unspoken question, Gabriel said, "I'm a lucky son of a gun to have a woman like Hermione at my side. Believe you me, I understand that fact very well."

"Any man would. She's a lovely young woman."

"Ain't she though! First time I saw her. . ." Goggins shook his head with remembered wonderment. "I sometimes ask myself. . ."

"What?"

"Well, it seems a marvel that a girl like her would have a fella' like me. I know I ain't the Adonis."

"But you beat out her other suitors?"

Goggins frowned. "Hermione's young and Agatha, that's her stepmother, guards her close."

"So the girl didn't have other suitors?"

"I'm not saying that. She's shy, don't say much when we're together. Leander says she's eager to tie the knot. Agatha says the same and I know they wouldn't lie. Oh, my luck turned the day I met Leander Mussman."

"So it seems," Oliver murmured.

As Goggins sailing canoe closed in on Middle Bass the conversation became less personal. He described the island where they were headed as shaped something like a duck minus the legs. The duck's neck formed East Point, a long narrow projection luxuriant with wild growths and picturesque with rough rocks and a tumbled beach. The tail of the duck was formed by the bobbed off western portion of the island. Upon this was located the grounds of the Middle Bass club.

"You'll be snowed under when you see that establishment," Goggins assured. "Buildings and improvements are first rate."

He shortened sail and Magic Carpet ghosted toward the main landing on the east side of the island. The boat had to compete for a mooring with numerous other vessels, including a dozen or so sailing canoes, rowboats and a steam launch.

"Are we late to the party?" Oliver asked.

Goggins looped one of Magic Carpet's lines around a piling and pointed at a group of men in formal dress. They were milling about in front of Wehrle's, a popular Middle Bass dance hall.

"We're right on time. See, there's some of our sailing fellas waiting to catch the next wagon to the club. The ladies are already here." Winking, he pointed at the damp cuffs on Oliver's trousers. "Didn't want to get their skirts wet. Not like us fellas who don't care about such tiff-toff."

A few minutes later they were on land. The wagon arrived and Oliver and Gabriel climbed aboard with the other canoe sailors. Under the darkening sky they were conveyed along an angling road cut through rich tracts of vineyard and orchard.

It was a merry group. The men shouted nautical compliments, playful insults, shared gossip, and talked of their campsites on Ballast. As they arrived at the grounds of the Middle Bass Club they agreed to race back to Ballast after the banquet ended.

The club's buildings were situated on a beautiful stretch of lakefront sheltered by natural forest. The complex included a club-house with a massive tower and wide verandahs. There was also a handsome pavilion and boat-house as well as a Gothic chapel and several well built cottages.

Goggins nudged Oliver in the ribs. "Didn't I say you'd be impressed?"

The wagon rolled up in front of a large hall obviously designed to hold club entertainments. Several ladies and gentlemen strolled on the lawn.

"There's Hermione," Gabriel exclaimed. Miss Mussman perched on a swing dangling from the branches of a towering oak. Her stepmother pushed her back and forth. With his eyes fixed on the pretty portrait the two females made, Gabriel scrambled out of the wagon. He stumbled over the wheel and Oliver grabbed his arm, saving him from an embarrassing fall.

Gabriel brushed himself off. "I know my fiancé wishes to thank you."

"She already has. We met in town this afternoon."

"Oh? In that case I'll just go and pay my respects. Have a look around. Enjoy yourself."

Gabriel hurried away and Oliver strolled toward the lakefront. He took in the soft summer air, the glow of the deepening evening light, and the musical lap of water against the pebbled beach.

Nearby men and women wandering about in handsome evening clothes made an idyllic picture. He felt as if he'd stepped into a parlor drawing, or perhaps into a summer version of the pretty little tableau captured in Chloe's glass ball. Long ago Oliver had learned that the reality pictured in parlor drawings and glass balls was not to be trusted.

"Ho there, Redcastle. Here's Reverend Mussman all agog to shake your hand."

Oliver turned. Gabriel, Leander Mussman and a woman in a green silk dress were headed toward him. The setting sun struck fire from the woman's red hair. It was Marietta. Her arm was tucked into Mussman's and she was smiling sweetly.

CHAPTER SEVEN

Leander Mussman seized Oliver's hand and squeezed it hard. "Redcastle, my dear, dear friend, at last we meet!"

Hermione's father was above average height. He had a robust figure set off by striped trousers and a beautifully tailored cutaway trimmed in pearl-gray silk.

Hermione had inherited her beauty from him. Even now in his middle years his fleshy, clean-shaven face was strikingly handsome. Silver hairs at his temples accented his combed back pouf of waving light brown locks. His unblinking pale blue gaze compelled attention while his deep, rich voice spilled into the ear like dark honey.

Oliver replied, "The pleasure is mine."

"My dear man, the pleasure is most totally my own. You have preserved the life of my child, a treasure more precious to me than the sapphires and rubies of India, more precious than the elixir of life itself."

"I'm glad the young lady suffered no harm. As for me, it was nothing."

"Nothing? Oh my dear dear chap, only a man with a core of tempered steel would make light of such a heroic deed! Indeed, to me your gallant plunge into the unplumbed waters of this great lake was an act of truly epic valor. My daughter is the bright silver moon of my starry night, a beacon in the wilderness of my beleaguered soul. Had she been swallowed by icy waters—"

He gestured dramatically at the waves lapping gently against the rock shore a few feet distant—"I would have been flung into an outer blackness of the psyche. Only the knowledge that I would soon join her in silvery Elysian fields would save me from a cataclysmic insanity of grief."

With Oliver's hand still captured firmly between his, he added, "But I'm neglecting my solemn duties as a host. Let me introduce my companion, the lovely Miss Marietta Dumont."

Marietta put out her hand and smiled coquettishly. "Pleased to meet you, Mr. Redcastle."

Oliver stared into Marietta's glinting green eyes. "Your name is familiar. Haven't I heard it before?"

"Possibly."

"Pshaw!" Mussman's opulent laugh oozed over them. "Of course you've heard the divine appellation of Marietta Dumont. This exquisite creature is a world famous actress. We are fortunate that Miss Dumont has agreed to grace the island of Put-In-Bay. Tomorrow night she is to perform a featured role in one of Shakespeare's most delightful comedies. I look forward to it with baited breath."

Marietta tapped Mussman's arm. "Leander, if you go on in this way Mr. Redcastle will think me immodest. I am not so famous as you claim. There are many, many actresses much better known than poor little me."

"But none lovelier or more talented! No, no, don't contradict me." He struck a pose. "On that I have taken a stand!"

A young man hurried up and whispered earnestly into Mussman's ear. The preacher straightened and patted Marietta's hand. "My dear, much to my regret I must excuse myself from your and Mr. Redcastle's delightful company. I'm afraid that I've been called to attend to some sadly mundane business. Why don't you and Hermione's heroic savior get better acquainted?"

"Yes," Oliver said. "Why don't we do that?"

When their host was no longer within hearing, he leaned forward and added, "Start by telling me what you're doing here. Are you and that oily-tongued slicker in cahoots?"

"Cahoots?" She rolled her eyes. "You see plots and schemes everywhere you look, don't you Ollie? I'm sorry to disappoint you, but Leander and I are merely old friends. He was a leading man in the first theatrical company I joined."

"I should have guessed. Were the two of you lovers?"

Marietta smiled archly. "I do believe you're jealous. No, Leander and I were never lovers, though I happen to know that he's had more than his share."

"I can imagine."

"That I doubt. Once a preacher's son, always a preacher's son. I don't suppose you ever had more than one lover at a time."

Oliver kept silent and Marietta shrugged. "Leander never confined himself to one woman. At least not in his heyday on the stage. In his youth he was one of the handsomest men in theater. Women buzzed around him like bees at a hive. He had his pick, and all of them were far more attractive than the stick of a woman he's calling his wife." She shot a scornful glance across the lawn at Agatha Mussman.

Oliver said, "He may have been a leading man with a flock of panting females trailing after him, but he's a Bible-banging fraud now."

"He's not a fraud. He's an actor."

"There's a difference? He's a long-winded swindler! This religious outfit of his is nothing but a scam. He enriches himself by spinning a web of nonsense, telling his followers he's had angelic visitations."

"Listen to you! You sound like a narrow-minded moralist. From what I've heard Leander does a great deal of good in this world. He feeds the hungry, gives men who've lost everything a purpose. So what if those who contribute to his cause are seduced by his charm? They're rich and can afford it. Besides, Leander's preachings may be fanciful but they're not lies."

"How's that possible? He claims to have been visited by an angel."

Marietta shrugged. "All actors believe their lines while speaking them. That's part of what made Leander such an effective Casanova. When he told women he loved them he believed it. Never mind that often as not he would leave them in the lurch the next day."

"How appropriate that Mussman's trying to buy a place called Gull Island. You admit he's putting on a show for the gullible fools he swindles?"

Marietta shrugged again. "I'm here to have dinner with the man and talk over old times, not to judge him. For all I know he really is having angelic visitations. Speaking of which, what are you doing on Middle Bass?"

"Same as you, having dinner."

"Oh pish! It can't be purely social. Nothing you do ever is. You must be investigating a crime. What does it have to do with poor Leander? Has he stolen a purse?"

"I'm not going to discuss my work with you."

"Then why should I discuss my friends with you? Oh look, here's Hermione. Isn't she the prettiest little thing you've ever seen in your life? It's a shame that she can't draw a free breath without that dragon of a stepmother hanging over her. I feel quite sorry for the child."

Hermione floated up to them. After the briefest nod to Oliver, she focused her large blue eyes on Marietta and held out her gloved hand. "Oh, Miss Dumont, when Papa told me you were coming I was thrilled beyond words. Years ago he took me to see you in 'The Lady and the Robber.' I do so look forward to your performance tomorrow night. Papa has promised to take me."

Agatha Mussman appeared behind the girl. In contrast to her pretty stepdaughter's pink muslin dress embroidered with rosebuds she wore steel gray silk with a neckline clamped around her throat by a thin band of silver lace. She'd squeezed her hair into a tight bun and her face even tighter with disapproval. How had such a drab woman managed to trap a flamboyant peacock like Leander, Oliver wondered. He speculated that her bank balance must have been very large indeed.

She thumped Hermione's shoulder. "Your papa was wrong to make that absurd promise. His duties will not allow him to waste time on a godless theatrical."

Marietta said, "Shakespeare's Midsummer Night's Dream has nothing to do with religion. It's a fantasy set in ancient Greece."

"That's exactly my point, godless and pagan. You play an immoral fairy who consorts with a donkey, do you not, Miss Dumont?"

Marietta's voice turned icy. "I play the lead role of Titania, if that's what you mean."

"That's exactly what I mean." The two women glared at each other.

Hermione shot a rebellious glance at her stepmother. "Papa will not renege on a promise to me." She seized Marietta's hand. "Let us sit next to each other at the banquet, Miss Dumont. I do so want to talk to you about the theater."

Agatha snapped, "Please recall that name cards have already been placed to determine seating."

Marietta drew Hermione out of her stepmother's clutch. "Then we must hurry and rearrange them, mustn't we!" Giggling conspiratorially, the two females skipped across the lawn toward the banquet hall while Agatha scowled after them.

Oliver said, "Your stepdaughter is very young. It's not surprising that she would be fascinated by Miss Dumont's glamour."

"You call it glamour? Well, I call it something else and I do not approve."

"I was surprised to meet the lady here. She and your husband appear to be on good terms."

Agatha eyed him coldly. "I'm not jealous of Marietta Dumont's coarse beauty, if that's what you're implying. Leander knew her in his acting days. That was long ago, when he was a different person in an altogether different life."

"Yet it's obvious you don't like her."

"Why should I think well of such a creature? She's pushed her way into our circle and is a bad influence on Hermione, for whom I stand in place of a mother."

"Hermione's father does not reject his old acquaintance. Indeed, they seem very friendly."

"So you've already pointed out. You do not understand Leander, Mr. Redcastle. He is a holy man, a visionary. He sees the good in everyone. Christ, you will remember, suffered Mary Magdalene to wash his feet."

"An interesting allusion."

"Excuse me, I must see to the arrangements in the hall. I am responsible for Hermione and must oversee her actions. She is a sweet girl but she can be thoughtless. I cannot allow her to change the seating. As you might imagine, a great deal depends on this banquet!"

"Acquiring Gull island means a lot to you?"

"Everything! The entire future of our holy community hangs in the balance!" Agatha picked up her skirts and stalked off.

A few minutes later the doors of the banquet hall were thrown open and the people gathered on the lawn began moving toward them. A wagon pulled up and a stately gentleman with a long white beard climbed out of it. Oliver recognized Jay Cooke, the famous financier and owner of Gibralter island.

Leander Mussman escorted him and his half dozen family members into the hall. Behind them the other guests streamed into the building.

Most were dressed in proper evening clothes, the men in cutaways and the ladies in long pastel summer gowns. The one standout, a man with a thick blond moustache, wore a light colored rather oddly tailored Norfolk jacket. Oliver recognized him and his companion. He followed the two inside and took advantage of the confusion in the hall to rearrange the name cards.

When the hubbub in the banquet room finally subsided, he took a seat next to them and introduced himself. The man in the Norfolk jacket replied in a German accent that he was Emil Venator. "So," he exclaimed, "I meet the famous Mr. Redcastle."

"Famous?"

The German pointed at the head table where Hermione sat whispering into Marietta Dumont's ear. The two females made a striking picture, Hermione's youthful loveliness in contrast to Marietta's ripe beauty. They, too, had succeeded in changing the place cards despite Agatha Mussman's objections.

Venator said, "But my dear fellow, the whole world of America knows how you rescued the exquisite Mussman princess from the watery grave. It's all over the island what a hero walks among us. As for me, why I was so fortunate to be a passenger on the steamship Hayes. I had the privilege to see it with my own eyes when you took your valiant plunge. A fine sight it was, very fine!"

Oliver replied, "I'm no hero. Anyone would have done the same."

"Not I. Much as I should hate to see a lovely lady drown, I'm only comfortable underground, not under the water."

At Oliver's raised eyebrows Venator added with a chuckle, "Ach, you see, I'm a miner not a sailor. I've crossed the ocean to climb into holes, not to take a swim."

"Really? Are you a follower of Reverend Mussman's?"

Venator laughed loudly, showing a mouthful of large teeth. "Not at all. This is the extremist I'm following!" He pointed at the bearded gentleman to his left. It was the man named Brown that Oliver had met when he'd rescued Hermione.

During his conversation with Venator Oliver had been glancing at Brown, tantalized again by an odd sense of familiarity. He had seen him, of course, on the steamship. But he felt certain they'd met at some prior time and had a feeling that the encounter was significant. He asked, "Do I know you?"

Venator tapped his friend's arm and winked at Oliver. "Oh, I think you may have heard this fellow's name. Let me make the introduction of one American hero to another. Mr. Oliver Redcastle meet Mr. John Brown Junior."

CHAPTER EIGHT

When Oliver recovered from his surprise he said, "You will not remember, Mr. Brown, but we met many years ago in Kansas."

"Indeed?"

"I was a boy at the time. My parents had settled in Lawrence."

"Abolitionists?"

"Yes. My father was preaching in the cause when he met my mother in Baltimore. She came from a family of wealthy southern sympathizers."

"She must have married against their wishes."

"Very much so, and consigned herself to a life of poverty by doing so."

"A worthy woman. Are your parents still alive?"

"Murdered along with my younger brothers in Quantrill's raid."

Brown replied gravely, "This land will ever be tainted by the blood spilled over the great sin of slavery. I, too, lost brothers in the cause. But tell me, how did we meet?

"My folks took me to your father's camp." Oliver remembered vividly how John Brown, surrounded by his handsome sons, had spoken against the pro-slavery forces flooding into Kansas. The fiery self-appointed warrior of God had whipped the crowd into a fighting frenzy. That had been before Brown sacrificed himself and his followers at Harpers Ferry and helped ignite the flames of civil war.

"I'm honored to meet you," Oliver said.

Brown Junior laughed without humor. "A disposition not universally shared. There are still those who would like to see me in the grave with my father. Did you fight for the Union?"

Oliver nodded. He didn't explain that he'd been McClellan's sharpshooter assigned to pick off Rebel commanders. He took no pride in that part of his service.

Brown said with a touch of bitterness, "I volunteered but they wouldn't have me. Nobody wanted to serve with John Brown's notorious son. That's why I and my brother settled on these islands."

"Choosing the area for its isolation from the mainland?"

"Exactly. Strangers are quickly identified on these isles. Enemies easily neutralized." Brown's gaze had turned enigmatic.

Oliver wondered how many threats the man had been forced to neutralize. During the war and after he and his family members would surely have been targets of southern sympathizers. Perhaps they still were. "I've heard that visitors to the island disappear occasionally."

Brown nodded. "We have had some mysterious disappearances."

"Someone mentioned a couple of men vanishing last year under peculiar circumstances."

"True enough. They were visiting the island to make plans for an encampment, a reunion of Johnson Island prisoners. When they disappeared the encampment was called off. They never turned up and nobody found their bodies. Most likely they went boating and drowned."

Oliver remembered that Waterman had expressed a similar view. Were they right, or was there more to the story? Brown seemed to read his mind.

"Mr. Redcastle, I assure you I had nothing to do with that occurrence. I'm a peaceable man."

"Except when provoked?"

"Except when sorely provoked. Fortunately, I haven't been sorely provoked in many years."

"I'm delighted to hear that. You mentioned your brother?"

"Owen. He's equally innocent of any violent action toward strangers. In fact Owen spends most of his time on Gibralter and has little occasion to mix with visitors to Put-In-Bay. He's Jay Cooke's caretaker."

"Did you have occasion to see these two men before they vanished so inexplicably?"

Brown shook his head. "I rarely stray from the bosom of my family and the confines of my property."

During this exchange, Emil Venator's bright, inquisitive eyes had darted between Oliver's face and Brown's. He slapped Brown on the back.

"To hear this man talk you'd think him a hermit. No such thing! He's a salesman with a tongue of silver. Why else would I have crossed an ocean to spend days crawling through caves?"

Oliver was about to ask what Venator meant when the first course, a "Consommé Royal," was placed in front of him. The attendant bending down to deliver it whispered, "Meet me out back after Mussman quits yapping."

The voice was Waterman's. He'd got himself employed waiting banquet tables for the evening, suggesting to Oliver that there must be a serious dearth of wait-staff on the island. He gave him the barest of nods and reached for his soupspoon.

A parade of dishes followed the consommé: filet of sole tartare, filet of beef with mushrooms, potatoes, various vegetables and quails on toast. After a lettuce salade the diners cleared their palates with champagne.

During the feast Oliver learned that John Brown Junior lived on Put-In-Bay's south shore. Though he made his living as a surveyor, he was something of a Renaissance man--interested in Geometry, Phrenology, Metaphysical Science and Geology. He and Emil Venator were investigating South Bass's rich veins of strontium with the notion of possibly going into business mining the mineral.

"I gather you've spent quite a bit of time exploring these caves," Oliver remarked.

"Ach, we certainly have!" Venator exclaimed. "I arrived yesterday and have hardly seen daylight since. We've been a pair of moles."

Brown laughed at this exaggeration. "It's not so bad as that, but we have been spending a lot of time underground."

"With more to come," Venator said. "This South Bass island is a limestone sponge riddled with caves."

"Are they interesting?" Oliver inquired politely.

"Oh, most interesting! And not just for the strontium crystals. This morning we found bones!"

"Bones?"

"Old ones," Brown chimed in. "Nothing to do with the disappearances we discussed earlier. These bones, I daresay, were from the Indians who were displaced by the white man."

"There's evidence that people have lived in the caves?"

"The caves maintain a constant temperature. It's not surprising that humans would find shelter in them from time to time," Brown commented.

Venator chuckled. "Recently, too. Yesterday we found signs that someone had been camping in the cave they call "Mammoth.""

"Really!" Oliver leaned forward. "What kind of signs?"

"Clothing, charred wood, a blanket. So not every tourist wants to pay for a hotel room." He chuckled.

"I'd like to visit some of these caves and see for myself."

Seemingly gratified by Oliver's interest Brown invited him to his house to view his collection of geological artifacts and do a spot of caving. Oliver quickly accepted.

Meanwhile he kept an eye on the other tables in the dining room. Marietta and Hermione Mussman still had their heads together, pausing in their chitchat only occasionally to sample one of the menu items placed before them.

Oliver saw Waterman position himself behind Marietta so that he could peer down into her cleavage while he replaced uneaten "Potatoes Duchesse" with a dish of string beans. Looking up, he caught Oliver's eye and winked lasciviously.

Finally Neapolitan ice cream was served followed by cakes, cheese, and fruit. Gabriel Goggins threaded his way through waiters pouring tea and coffee out of silver pots. Watching him strut to the podium Oliver was reminded of an overfed pigeon puffing his feathers for approval.

Candlelight gleamed on his round face as he proudly introduced Leander Mussman to the banqueters. After describing him as "our gracious host," and "a holy man who has come to these islands with a proposal that deserves your generous attention," he turned the lectern over to the charismatic religious leader.

* * *

An hour later Oliver slipped outside. A full moon washed the night. Soft insect wings brushed his face. He heard the drone of cicadas and smelled the acrid burn of cigarette smoke. As he rounded the banquet hall he saw the hot red glow of a lit match and the shape of a man slouched against a porch rail.

"Waterman?"

"Thought you'd never get here. Thought that fool, Mussman, would never stop jawing. You'd think a fella' could put on a feed like that wouldn't have to beg for money."

"I doubt Mussman paid for tonight's banquet."

"'Course not. Jay Cooke footed the bill. That man's a fool for preachers. Wines and dines 'em over to his island all the time." Waterman snorted. "Maybe I should take up bible-thumping. Might be an easier way to earn my bread than what I'm doing for you."

"I'd be interested to hear what you are doing for me."

"Ain't it obvious? I'm slinging hash so's I can pick up the tittle-tattle."

"I hope you didn't invite me back here just to complain. What have you learned?"

"I learned that fool preacher expects every rich man this side of New York City to give him money to buy his own private island. Wants to set up his idea of paradise. And what would that be? Why, a place where he can pen up a bunch of poor people and boss them around."

Oliver had much the same opinion. Mussman was a megalomaniac. He talked about "creating a community of God set apart from the worldly temptations of the mainland." Oliver suspected that the Mussmans wanted to purchase Gull Island so they could rule their own private kingdom. Was it more Leander's idea or Agatha's, he wondered. And what did Hermione think about being immured on Gull island with her bossy stepmother? Was the prospect of that why she'd thrown herself off the R.B. Hayes?

Louise Titchener

Oliver said, "You don't need to tell me about Mussman's speech. I sat through it, too. What about Aballo?"

"Ain't no sign of your bankrobber."

"Get anything on the Mussman girl? If Aballo were here he'd try to get in touch."

"I followed that bit of fluff half the day. Walked my feet off going from the shops to the diving horse show to the waterslide and back. Plenty of young bucks showed signs of wanting to sniff up her skirts. The old biddy guarding her didn't let any of them near."

"You mean her stepmother, Agatha."

"Is that her name? Suits her. That's what I'd name an old cat with bald spots. Good for catching rats and nothing else."

"So you've got nothing for me."

"I earned my pay. Ain't my fault you're barking up the wrong tree. Aballo ain't the fool you take him for. Man's not here."

"What about the island's caves? Could he be hiding in one of them?"

"Not likely. Only a true islander would know where to hide in a cave." Waterman tossed away the stub of his cigarette and walked back inside the banquet hall.

Oliver contemplated the red sparks glowing in the grass. So far his association with Waterman had been more irritating than useful. Why had William Pinkerton set him up with the difficult fellow?

Shrugging, he started back toward the front of the building. When he arrived at the door he kept walking, drawn by the sound of the waves dashing against the rocks. The wind had come up. It occurred to him that tonight's passage back to Put-In-Bay would not be smooth. By now the rug carpeting Goggins' sailboat was probably waterlogged.

The moon vanished behind a rag of cloud. When it reappeared it outlined a man and a woman beneath a tree at the shoreline. They spread their arms, flew at each other and embraced passionately. The man covered the woman's face with kisses. The woman seemed to melt into his body.

Oliver was about to turn away, embarrassed at spying on their intimacy when he realized that the female looked familiar. It was Hermione Mussman.

CHAPTER NINE

Wind carried the sound of Oliver's pounding feet. The man drew back from the woman, lifted his head and gazed in Oliver's direction like a prairie dog scenting a fox. The moon vanished behind a cloud. When it reappeared Hermione stood alone.

Oliver dashed past her and along the water's edge. At first he thought he heard the sound of running feet. Then he heard nothing but the wind. He searched until jumbled rocks and vegetation made the shoreline impassible. He squinted into the darkness. Shadowy trees and the glint of moonlight on restless water were all he saw. He listened hard but heard only the rising wind and the lake's rhythmic gurgle and slap.

Hermione had headed toward the security of the banquet hall. He caught up with her in front of the closed double doors.

"Where is he?"

"Take your hands off me!" She tried to pull free but he tightened his grasp.

"That was Frank Aballo with you just now, wasn't it!"

"I don't know what you're talking about. Unhand me or I'll scream!"

"You know, of course, that you're consorting with a wanted man, a thief."

"Who do you think you are? Pulling me out of the water doesn't give you the right to spy on me! You have no rights over me!"

"Does your father know Aballo's followed you here? I think not."

The doors of the hall crashed open and Agatha Mussman rushed out. "What are you doing Mr. Redcastle? How dare you restrain Hermione in this atrocious manner! Release her at once!"

Oliver let go of the girl who fell weeping into her stepmother's arms. The two returned to the banquet hall. Before they disappeared Agatha shot Oliver a poisonous glance.

Marietta materialized out of the darkness. Slapping Oliver's arm with her folded fan she commented acidly, "I didn't know you fancied girls so young. Really, Olly, that child could be your daughter."

"She's not my daughter and I don't fancy her."

"Then you must be made of stone. Every man here has an itch for the chit. It's those big blue eyes and winsome golden ringlets."

Marietta's features were lost in shadow, but Oliver could see her hair outlined by moonlight. The wind loosened tendrils from her topknot and lifted loose curls off her forehead. Her scent wafted to him. He said, "On what do you base your observation? Did you see someone in particular follow her outside?"

"No."

"You gossiped with the girl all through the banquet. Did Hermione say anything to you about a lover?"

"She has a fiancé. He introduced her father's speech."

"It's not Gabriel Goggins I'm talking about."

"What are Hermione Mussman's love affairs to you? Is that why you're here? To spy on the romantic foibles of a seventeen-year-old?"

"It's more than foibles. She's involved with a bank robber named Frank Aballo."

Marietta's mouth opened, but for several seconds no sound came forth. Finally, she laughed softly. "Really? How very interesting. That's why you're camped on Put-In-Bay? To catch Hermione Mussman's bank-robber lover?"

"My reasons for being here are no business of yours."

"Haven't you learned by now that it's foolish to cut off your nose to spite your face?"

"Meaning?"

"Meaning that I can easily make your reasons for being here into my business. Hmmmm. In fact, very easily. For instance, like father like daughter."

"In what respect?"

"Hermione nourishes a secret infatuation with the stage. Tonight she talked of little else. I fear the poor motherless girl has few women friends in which she can confide. Perhaps that's why she prattled on so artlessly to poor little me."

"Are you saying she mentioned Aballo?"

"No, but I have little doubt I could draw her out on almost any subject. That is, if I had a good reason to do so." Marietta smiled up at him sweetly.

He said, "You're proposing to worm information out of Hermione Mussman in return for money?"

"I'm a poor struggling actress. Any payment you might choose to give me for undertaking such unpleasant work would be welcome. But that's not what I really want. You know very well what I want, Oliver." Her silky voice hardened. "Time with my daughter."

He snapped, "You abandoned Chloe like an unwanted kitten."

"Only because I had no choice. I'm her mother, and she needs me. If not now, then later. Give me what I want, Oliver, and I'll help you catch your bank-robber."

Half an hour later most of Leander Mussman's guests stood in knots on the lawn waiting patiently for transportation to the Middle Bass dock. Stomachs full and well-watered with claret and champagne, they chatted amiably. As the wagons carted them away laughter echoed through the darkness. Oliver and Gabriel Goggins were among the last to leave.

While Oliver waited for Goggins to finish his business inside the banquet hall, he looked in back of the building for Gene Waterman. But he had disappeared into the kitchen and couldn't be talked to without exciting comment. As Oliver returned to the front of the building Goggins materialized.

"So, there you are, Redcastle! Capital evening, wouldn't you say? Hope you enjoyed it. Know you got a good feed."

"The food was excellent."

"And plenty of it!" Goggins slapped Oliver on the back. "Leander's not a man to scrimp when it comes to doing right by his guests. Hope they remember that and loosen their purse-strings for him."

"You said it was your job to persuade them to contribute to Mussman's project. Do you think you were successful?"

"We'll know soon enough."

"How much support is there for the establishment of a religious community on Gull Island?"

Goggins' brow creased and he lowered his voice. "Mixed, I'm afraid. Jay Cooke likes the idea. He agrees it might temper some of the ungodliness of the islanders. Partying, drinking on the Sabbath." Contemplating this wickedness on Put-In-Bay, Gabriel shook his head.

Oliver kept his jaws clamped together. Judging from the banquet they'd just enjoyed it seemed to him that Cooke and Mussman were not strangers to excess themselves.

An empty wagon rolled up and the two men climbed aboard. At the dock they found Leander Mussman waving away the last departing steam launch filled with his guests. Several canoes maneuvered around it, their sails flapping loudly.

"Ready for more adventure?" Goggins shouted into the wind.

"Are we really sailing back to Put-In-Bay in this gale?"

"Gale? Why, man, you're not afraid of a bit of a blow are you?"

Oliver peered at the sky. Streamers of cloud raced across the moon's face. Below his feet water pounded at the wooden dock. Goggins canoe lurched sickeningly at its mooring. He said, "I've heard storms on Lake Erie can shoot up like geysers and blow you away."

"All the more fun for sailing fellas like us. Right Leander?"

Smoothing back the hair whipping around his forehead, Leander said, "My dear Gabriel, I have perfect confidence in your nautical skills." His rich voice was slurred. It was obvious that he'd imbibed more than his share of champagne.

Goggins snubbed the canoe to a piling and clambered awkwardly into it. Oliver followed. He'd been right about the rug. It squelched wetly under his shoes.

Once the craft had stopped see-sawing, he offered his hand to Mussman. Despite his inebriated condition, the charismatic preacher managed to step into the boat without overturning it.

John Brown Junior and Emil Venator emerged from the darkness and sprinted to the dock.

"Wait, wait!" Brown shouted. He explained that they'd decided to walk back from the banquet hall and had lost track of time. Since they'd missed the steam launch could they beg a ride back in Gabriel's sailing canoe?

The vessel was already overloaded. Oliver expected Goggins' to suggest some alternative. Instead he cheerfully assented and the two men struggled into the sailboat. When it finally righted itself they cleared the harbor, the wind howling at their backs and the Magic Carpet's sail straining like an overfilled bladder.

CHAPTER TEN

Out on the open water the boat wallowed and plunged. Gabriel shouted, "Glad the ladies went back under power! Bit dicey out here!"

Oliver thought "hair-raising" was a more apt description of their situation. "Have you got life preservers aboard?"

Goggins' pointed at a heap of shapeless waterlogged objects.

"How many?"

"Three."

Venator rolled his pale eyes in obvious disgust. Wind-blown water plastered his hair to his narrow skull. Behind him Brown looked equally grim and bedraggled. His soaked dinner jacket hung on his solid frame like a wet bedsheet.

"We'll not need life preservers," Goggins protested. "Magic Carpet is a good old girl. Never fear, she'll see us through a spot of rough weather."

His voice could barely be heard over the roaring wind. Soon after they'd left the dock the sky had turned leaden and the wind had exploded with unbelievable fury. Now it howled around their ears, whipping the waves into greater and greater ferocity.

They'd managed to shorten sail, but that had not stabilized the overloaded canoe's sickening rolls. Leander, despite his earlier expressed confidence, crouched in the stern moaning piteously. He had already vomited a quantity of food and alcohol over the side.

At first the Magic Carpet had not been alone on the rough water. It had been accompanied by a half dozen other sailing canoes belonging to members of the American Canoe Association racing each other back to their camp on Ballast Island. Goggins, clearly a poorer sailor than his racing colleagues, had not been able to keep up with them. In any case he would have veered from the pack to drop Oliver, Brown, Venator and Leander Mussman off at Put-In-Bay. Now Magic Carpet was alone on the storm-tossed lake.

Goggins wrestled the tiller while Oliver, Brown and Venator bailed furiously. Wet to the skin and half blinded by water driven like nails by the hammering wind, Oliver clenched his teeth in a vain effort to keep them from chattering. His shoes and socks clung to his skin like leaches and his hands were scraped raw.

Whimpering, Leander began to vomit again. At that moment the bucking craft plunged into a trough. Water poured over the preacher's head. Oliver, Brown and Venator bailed like madmen, heaving bucketful after bucketful of Lake Erie over the side only to have it whip back into their faces.

Brown muttered, "This is exactly how people disappear around here. They're drowned in a squall. Erie's bottom is paved with bones."

Venator gave a cry of alarm and pointed. Squinting through needles of spray Oliver thought he saw the dim outline of a sail coming at them.

Goggins shouted, "Sail, ho! Watch out, man!"

The raging wind had barely ripped the words from his lips when the rogue vessel clipped the forward edge of the canoe. Over the screaming wind Oliver heard the painful shriek of splintering wood. The boat pitched violently and Oliver and Leander Mussman were thrown out of one side while Brown and Venator were flung from the other. Goggins, clinging to the tiller, disappeared into a wall of water.

Oliver surfaced. A shred of cloth brushed his hand and he seized it. The cloth turned out to be the tail of Leander Mussman's frockcoat belling around his struggling body. Another wave rolled over his and Oliver's heads. Sputtering and gasping Oliver fought free. Mussman had disappeared. Oliver yanked at the tail of the preacher's waterlogged coat and dragged him back above water. He had gone limp and appeared unconscious.

Wrapping an arm under the man's chin Oliver fought to stay afloat. He looked around for Brown and Venator but saw only heaving black water. He shouted their names. Once he thought he received an answering cry. After that he heard nothing but wind an occasional crack of thunder.

Despite his fleshy physique Leander Mussman showed no inclination to float. Weighed down by his heavy clothing, his large head continually sinking under the water as if it were a lead bowling ball, he became a dangerous anchor. Another wave swamped Oliver and something hit him in the elbow. It was one of the kapok life preservers that had been in the bottom of Goggins boat.

For what seemed like hours Oliver clung to it with one arm while he endeavored to hold Mussman's heavy head above water. As quickly as it had come up the wind died down. The water calmed. Eventually the clouds parted and a scattering of stars pierced the night sky. On his right he saw a few lights twinkling on what he judged to be land. He started to kick in that direction. Chilled, exhausted, and burdened with Mussman's dead weight he thought he had little chance of reaching it.

He was afraid of slipping into unconsciousness and drowning. For the sake of his own survival he considered abandoning the preacher. For all he knew the man was already drowned. He showed no sign of life. Yet simply letting go of him to save his own skin went against the grain. Oliver decided to try and hold on a little longer.

A few minutes later he succumbed to temptation and closed his eyes. Mussman slipped from his grasp and began to float away. Jerked awake. Oliver grabbed the sinking preacher's collar and dragged him back up above the waterline. Nearby a light bobbed on the lake's black surface. Oliver croaked, "Help! Help!"

"Ho there! Who's that?" Oars splashed. A boat rowed by a shadowy figure emerged from the darkness. The lantern fixed to its prow cast a blinding halo.

"Help! Help me!"

The boat pulled alongside. "Glad to offer my assistance," the man inside said. "Owen Brown at your service."

CHAPTER ELEVEN

A fiendish carpenter hammered rusty nails inside Oliver's skull. His eyes were balls of flame. Every joint and muscle of his body hurt, and he had no idea where he was.

A thunderous explosion jerked him out of bed and onto his feet. He stumbled to the narrow window opposite and peered out on a spectacular vista of blue water studded with craggy rocks.

A door opened behind him. "Awake are you? Suppose Cooke's cannon blew you off my mattress."

"Cannon?"

Owen Brown stood in the open doorway. A slender, wiry man of indeterminate age, he wore shirtsleeves and rough brown pants held up by suspenders. After pulling Leander Mussman and Oliver from the lake he had offered them shelter in his cottage.

Oliver asked, "Mussman?"

"Preacher's still breathing but otherwise dead to the world and looks to stay that way for a spell." Owen shook his head. "I fear he may have taken serious harm from that Lake Erie swimming lesson. Man's in the next room. See for yourself."

Oliver followed his host into another small bedroom. Leander had been unconscious when they'd carried him from Owen Brown's rowboat. Owen had worked for a good half hour at pumping water from his lungs.

Man's about as responsive as a dead catfish," he had declared when a puddle had finally dribbled from Leander's blue lips. Together they'd stripped off the preacher's wet clothing, wrapped him in a flannel blanket and put him to bed. Oliver had hoped that by morning he would be awake. This was not the case.

Looking like a pasty ghost of himself, Mussman lay inert on a narrow iron bedstead. Oliver listened to his frayed breathing and then looked at Owen. "What do you think?"

John Brown Junior's younger brother shrugged. Behind his beard he had the handsome, ascetic features that characterized the other members of his family. His eyes, however, had a haunted look that made him appear both more vulnerable and less approachable. He said, "Time will tell. Doesn't it always? Cooke's got a sawbones on the way."

"That's good. What about your brother?"

"John and his German friend made it back to Put-In-Bay all right. After I dropped you here, I rowed over to make sure."

"Gabriel Goggins? He was at the helm when we were hit."

"Don't know. We'll hear today."

Another burst of cannon fire made Oliver jump.

Owen smiled. "The old man likes to set off his gun when distinguished guests arrive. We just got such a visitor. You might recognize the name. Ulysses S. Grant?"

"President Grant?" Oliver rubbed his throbbing temples. "President Ulysses S. Grant is here on Jay Cooke's private island?"

"Grant's not president now nor ever will be again. Man's penniless and deathly sick. Throat cancer."

"Good Lord! Grant's troubles never seem to end. I heard he got swindled on Wall Street."

"Picked clean by the money vultures. Hopes to regroup by publishing his memoirs. Cooke invited him here for some peace and quiet so he could get started writing on them." Owen crossed to a window and stood looking out, his angular face bathed in morning sunshine. "Wonder how much peace and quiet he's going to find around this place. Not much to be had last night."

Oliver said, "I owe you my life."

"You already thanked me."

"I want to thank you again."

"No need. You weren't far from shore when I fished you out of the water. Another few yards and you'd been able to walk onto Gibralter."

"Not Mussman."

"No." They both looked toward the immobile figure on the bed. Owen said, "He'll need nursing. Cooke sent word to the wife. Meantime, you can get some breakfast."

The two men left the caretaker's cottage and walked up a path that meandered to Jay Cooke's imposing summer residence. Beyond the cliff at Oliver right shoulder the sun sparkled on the water. Masts filled the harbor, bobbing in a gentle breeze. The lake looked friendly, even inviting. It looked as if one could easily swim to Put-In-Bay.

Cooke's limestone mansion climbed three stories from the highest spot on his tiny gem of an island. A tower soared above it, adding almost half as much height. Squinting up, Oliver speculated that it must command a fabulous view of the lake and surrounding islands.

Owen commented that another man named Oliver had found it so. From a lookout just across the lawn from the mansion Oliver Hazard Perry was supposed to have first sighted the English war ships that he defeated in the Battle of Lake Erie during the war of 1812.

Excepting a few downed branches there was no sign of last night's tempest. Late morning sunshine washed the grassy area between the cottage and the mansion. Miniature white butterflies fluttered amongst a variety of wildflowers sprouting from rocks close to the water. Oliver saw several small outbuildings and a vegetable garden. A bell began to toll.

"Call to morning prayers," Owen explained. "I'll have to go but you can stay behind and get your breakfast."

He pointed at the door to the kitchen, then hurried around to the front of the house. Oliver hesitated. Curiosity prevailed and he walked to the side of the house where he could see the family gathered in front of the porch.

Light filtering through tall trees dappled the top of Jay Cooke's gray hair and glinted off his long white beard. Earnestly, he read aloud from a prayer book. His household stood in a semicircle around him. Looking aged beyond his years, Ulysses S. Grant sat on a bench with his hands folded in his lap and his eyes closed.

Seeing the hero of his youth look so ill made Oliver take a step backward. Yet, he couldn't tear his gaze from the scene. It reminded him of his childhood. How often had he stood with his mother listening to his father read prayers in just that solemn tone of voice?

One of the women standing with her back to him and her head bowed could almost have been his mother. While he'd been floating in Lake Erie, expecting death, he'd thought of her. His father had been a difficult man who never hesitated to deliver a beating at the least sign of disobedience. Oliver's mother had been his refuge—the one bit of softness and comfort in his young life.

Repressing painful memories, he turned on his heel and headed for the kitchen. It was empty, the housekeeper having joined the Cooke family for prayers. Boiled eggs, a crockery bowl of strawberries and a plate of biscuits sat on the table along with honey and several kinds of jam. Until that moment Oliver hadn't realized how hungry he was. Last night's banquet seemed a thing of the distant past.

He helped himself to biscuits and eggs and had just downed a cup of coffee from a pot on the stove when the housekeeper returned. She was a cheerful looking woman with a broad forehead and light brown hair done up in a loose topknot.

"Awake at last, I see," she declared. "Mr. Redcastle, isn't it? I'm Anna McMeens. Terrible about that storm last night. I'm glad you're feeling chipper enough to eat."

She refilled his coffee cup and informed him that Leander's family had arrived with a doctor summoned from Port Clinton.

"Are they attending Leander now?"

"Doctor and the womenfolk are at Owen's cottage. I'm surprised you didn't hear the ruckus when they passed by."

Oliver downed the last of his coffee, thanked Mrs. McMeens and retraced his steps to the cottage. As he approached he heard raised female voices.

"Hussy!"

"Considering what sort of woman you are, dear Agatha, your abuse is pathetic!"

"How ridiculous! You can't fool me with your false airs! You're here to worm you way back into Leander's life by corrupting his poor innocent child. Well, I'm her mother and I won't stand for it!"

"I beg to differ. You are not her mother. In fact, you have no legal right over her whatsoever. And certainly none over me! As for corrupting influences, I'm nothing to match what you've been getting up to!"

"How dare you insult me!"

Oliver strode into Owen Brown's tiny parlor where Marietta and Agatha Mussman glared at each other. Agatha, in dull gray, balled her fists at her side. Marietta, in bright pink, planted her ruffled parasol into a crack in the floor and twirled it furiously. The dramatic contrast between their costumes made them appear like generals of opposing armies.

Hermione, looking pale and frightened, had pressed herself against a horsehair sofa. Owen Brown and a large red-faced man carrying a medical bag hung in the entry to Leander Mussman's bedroom witnessing the confrontation in round-eyed amazement.

The medical man exclaimed, "Ladies, please. I cannot allow this disturbance. We have a very sick man in this house!"

Agatha turned away from Marietta and begged, "Doctor Reno, say not that my poor husband is at death's door! Oh, please say it isn't so!"

The doctor looked grave. "Madam, I cannot deceive you. Due to the stress of his watery ordeal Reverend Mussman has suffered a brain hemorrhage and is in a state of suspended animation. He cannot be moved."

Agatha pressed her hands against her shallow bosom. "This is dreadful, terrible news. What are we to expect? Will he recover? Oh please tell me that he will!"

"In cases such as these there is no predicting the outcome. He may wake up perfectly well at any moment. Or he may linger in this vegetative state indefinitely. Only time will answer."

"What are we to do? Oh, what are we to do?" She turned to Hermione who had sunk into the sofa and covered her face with her hands.

The doctor made as if to pat Agatha's arm and then thought better of the contact. He said, "Since its best that Reverend Mussman not be moved, Mr. Owen Brown, here, has kindly agreed to let him remain at his cottage until he recovers. Or until it seem clear that he will not."

Agatha squared her bony shoulders. "He will recover! I'll pray for it night and day! Surely God would not be so cruel as to take our dear Leander from us!"

"He'll need constant nursing."

"Hermione and I will tend him night and day! Won't we, Hermione?"

The girl nodded dumbly.

"I'll help," Marietta interjected.

The doctor said a nervous thank you. He and Owen Brown beat a hasty retreat to the patient's room. When the two men were gone Agatha shot Marietta a scornful glance.

"Ridiculous! What can a woman like you do for Leander? I hope you're not going to offer to pray!"

Marietta snapped, "A man in his state needs more than prayers. I'll sit with him. I'll read to him."

"I suppose you imagine your voice will wake him from the dead." Agatha sniffed. "Won't you be far too busy flaunting yourself on the stage to spare Leander your precious time?"

"Little you know! I perform in the evening. I will be perfectly free during the day!"

"Then spend your daylight hours, such as they are, practicing your silly, foolish lines. Leander has no need of you and I will not allow you to visit him here." Gathering up her gray skirts, Agatha seized Hermione's arm. "Come along, we must see what we can do to make your sainted father comfortable."

After the girl was dragged away, Marietta glared at Oliver. "You've been standing there like a wooden Indian! Why didn't you say something?"

"What was I supposed to say?"

"A great deal more than you did! It was you who rescued Leander, after all."

"I kept his head above water. That doesn't give me any say in his care. Agatha is his wife, after all."

"So she says."

"What do you mean by that?"

"Never mind what I mean. If they're married it's only because of her money. It certainly can't be the loveliness of her person!"

"Regardless, it's her right to rule on who can and cannot visit his sickbed."

"Oh, pish!" Marietta stalked past him and into the sunlight.

Oliver followed her out of the cottage. "You can't be certain of Leander's reasons for marrying Agatha. Perhaps she has charms of which we are not aware."

"Ha!" Marietta snapped open her parasol. "You have only to look at that dried up prune. A leopard doesn't change its spots. Leander always courted beauties. I should know."

"Why? Were you his paramour?"

"No, but I knew women who were. They were nothing like Agatha, I can tell you that." She started down the hill.

"Where are you going?"

"To get some air. After being in that horrible woman's company all morning I need some oxygen."

He caught up with her. "How did you manage to come over with the doctor? How did you even know Leander was here?"

"Word gets around very fast on an island. Actually, Hermione told me. Her hotel room is only a few doors from mine."

"Hermione asked you to come to Gibralter?"

"She did. The poor girl hates that old witch as much as I'm beginning to. The woman is beyond rude. She actually barred my path onto the boat. I had to force my way past her."

Oliver suppressed a smile. "You must have been determined to come."

"Of course I was determined. Leander is a dear old friend."

"Was it friendship that brought you here or something else?"

She stopped dead in the path and whirled toward him. Her parasol cast her face into shadow. Only her full mouth, the tip of her nose and the rapid rise and fall of her bosom under its layer of pink ruffles were clearly visible. "Such as?"

"Last night you tried to make a bargain with me."

"Did I? Really? I wonder what it could have been. Jog my memory won't you Ollie?"

"You know very well that you offered to find out if Hermione Mussman is in contact with her lover."

"I take it you don't refer to Gabriel Goggins."

"Stop playing games. I'm talking about Frank Aballo. You implied that you would be willing to worm your way into the girl's confidence in exchange for a visit with Chloe. Obviously, you've done the former. Now I'm ready to consider the latter."

"You're willing to let me see Chloe?"

"I said I'd consider it."

"Consideration isn't good enough. I want your word that you're willing to let her know her mama is still alive? I want to be able to see my baby." She veered from the path and walked rapidly toward a small hill topped by a gazebo.

When Oliver caught up with her she was standing with her back to him, staring down at the lake. The wind plastered her skirts to her legs.

"All right," he said, "it's a deal."

She pointed at a cluster of boulders rising out of the water. "What's that?"

A dark object floated among them, slapping up against the huge, mossy stones with every wave that rolled in.

Oliver squinted into the hard sunlight. "My God, it's Gabriel Goggins!"

CHAPTER TWELVE

It was more than an hour before Oliver and Owen Brown succeeded in hoisting Gabriel's body to the dock. They lay the waterlogged corpse out on the cement and stood back. A commotion on the hill distracted their attention. Brown's cottage door banged open. Hermione dashed out closely followed by Marietta and Agatha.

Hermione's stepmother plucked at the girl's gauzy sleeve. "Oh, please, dearest, don't look!"

But Hermione did look. She screamed and sank to the ground.

Oliver left Owen guarding the corpse and trotted up to the cottage. Agatha seized his hand and implored, "Help us take her inside. Don't let her wake up and see that. . .that thing!"

He lifted the unconscious girl and carried her through the cottage door. After depositing her on a settee he watched as Marietta applied wet cloths to her forehead and Agatha set about reviving her with smelling salts. The women seemed, for the time being, to work as a team.

Seeing he was only in their way, he backed out of the room. On the dock he found Doctor Reno kneeling over Gabriel's corpse.

"What do you think happened?"

"Obviously, the poor fellow drowned."

Oliver pointed at a bruise purpling the side of Gabriel's head. "Perhaps not. The blow causing that could have killed him before he hit the water."

Reno shrugged. "The body was knocked about in the lake for hours. Nothing can be determined for certain until we take it to the mainland for a thorough examination."

"You mean an autopsy."

"That's right. I'll make arrangements." He shook out a blanket. As it settled over Gabriel's battered face Marietta hurried down the path.

She took Oliver aside. "What's going to happen now?"

"The doctor's going up to the main house to see about transporting Gabriel's body back to the mainland."

"I meant to Hermione."

"I've no idea. Is she conscious?"

"Yes, but she refuses to speak. All she does is lay moaning and shuddering. It's pitiful. The child's in no condition to get onto a boat, certainly not one containing the corpse of her fiancé. The poor girl is beside herself with grief."

"Perhaps."

"Perhaps what?"

"Perhaps it's grief."

"What else could it be?"

"There are any number of possibilities. Guilt, for instance."

"Guilt? Whatever do you mean?"

Oliver shrugged. "We both know Hermione wasn't in love with Gabriel Goggins. Doubtless, that's why she threw herself into the water the other day."

"Are you talking about the accident on the ferry where you played the rescuing hero?"

"No accident. That young woman didn't fall, she jumped. My guess is she threw herself into the lake out of despair at being trapped into an unwanted engagement. Or perhaps to punish her father for forcing her into the engagement. Now she's free. Gabriel is out of the picture."

They both looked at Gabriel's waterlogged remains abandoned under a blanket. It was a pathetic sight. Above it seabirds whirled and dived, crying out like lost souls.

"Poor boy," Marietta whispered. "I can hardly believe it. Last night he seemed so jolly, so full of life. Now he's just. . ."

"Just a piece of flotsam. He may have been a young fool, but he didn't deserve to be betrayed by the woman he loved and then drowned like an unwanted puppy."

Marietta stamped her foot. "You are the most cynical man in the world! You can't think the girl's happy to have her fiancé dead and her father at death's door."

"I don't suppose she fainted out of happiness, no."

"You agree she's heartbroken?"

"About Gabriel? Hardly. Frank Aballo, her bank robber lover, could console her and has every intention of doing so. I saw them in each other's arms on Middle Bass last night."

Marietta's eyebrows flew up. "If that's true how do you account for her present distress?"

"Haven't I already mentioned the word 'guilt'? If she's half as religious as she pretends her conscience has got to prick her now."

"You honestly think that girl bears a responsibility in all this tragedy?"

"I don't know but I plan to find out." Oliver seized Marietta's wrist and drew her close. "Before we spotted Gabriel's body in the water we had struck a bargain."

Her expression became shuttered. "I haven't forgotten."

"You said that if I let you see Chloe you'd befriend Hermione, find out about this bank robber. Are you still willing?"

"I'm willing to do anything to see my child again."

"Even spy on a friend?"

"Yes. Oh don't look at me like that! I know what you were thinking when you talked about Hermione's conscience. You think I've no conscience."

"Do you?"

"You've put me in a position where I can't afford one. If you really think I'm such an unscrupulous wretch why are you willing to bargain with me about Chloe?"

"Why indeed?" He was silent for a moment, breathing hard. "Gabriel Goggins was an innocent. I want to know who killed him and why."

"You wouldn't trade with me for Chloe if that were your only motive. You know she needs her mother. Admit it."

"All right, she needs a mother. It's just a pity the one she's got is you."

He regretted the words the moment they were out. Trying to ignore the wounded look in Marietta's eyes and the bitter taste in his mouth, he released her and stalked blindly up the hill. Why lash out at her like that, he asked himself. Why did he still harbor such violent feelings where she was concerned? He'd thought he'd put their disastrous love affair behind him. Apparently that wasn't so.

He ran into Doctor Reno and Jay Cooke discussing what should be done about Gabriel.

Cooke asked the physician, "Do you really think an autopsy will be necessary?"

"Under these circumstances, I'm afraid so. Does the deceased have family who should be contacted?"

"None that I know of. The parents are both dead. Gabriel was their only child. Except for his connection with the Mussmans the poor boy was alone in the world. This is a sad event."

The men made arrangements for the immediate transport of Gabriel's body. Before the hour was out Oliver accompanied Doctor Reno and the corpse to Put-In-Bay. He helped carry the dead young man onto a steamship destined for the mainland. While toting the heavily laden stretcher up the gangplank the blanket covering Gabriel's body curled in the wind, laying bare his shoeless feet. There was something infinitely dismal about the sight and Oliver looked away.

After he watched the steamship pull out into the harbor he returned to his hotel, changed clothes and headed for the Post Office. It was far too soon to expect a reply to the letter he'd sent Chloe. But he'd left a forwarding address in Chicago and had instructed his housekeeper, Mrs. Milawney, to write every three days.

He was pleased to discover an envelope addressed in her crabbed hand waiting for him. Before allowing himself to read it he went to the telegraph office fronting Doller's dock and picked up a telegram from William Pinkerton.

With both communications safe in his pocket Oliver walked to the park. It was a busy place. Groups of picnickers lounged about on the grass. Children hooted and screeched on swings. Near the fountain four young girls batted a tennis ball back and forth. He was lucky to locate an empty bench under a shady tree where he could peruse his mail.

Folded inside the missive from Mrs. Milawney was a small scrap of pink paper signed by Chloe.

Dear Papa, I hope you are well. Mrs. Miloney says you are going to ride the train all the way back home. I liked the train ride out here tho it was long. Tell Jimmy I wish he could be here to play. I kno he would like the horses and the cows. Our cabin is nice but it has spyders. I am lonely. My dollies are afraid of the cows but they like the horses. Love, Chloe

Oliver ran a finger over the childish handwriting. Jimmy was Mrs. Milawney's nephew. At this time of year the boy was doubtless working twelve-hour shifts in the canneries. Oliver wished he could have afforded to send Jimmy to Arizona to keep Chloe company. That had not been possible.

When he had first inherited his aunt's house and moved to Baltimore he'd envisioned himself living quietly, retired from the stress of his years as a Pinkerton operative. Unfortunately, the return on his investments had proved disappointing. To increase his income he'd turned to the only trade he knew. But the process of establishing a new private detection agency in Baltimore had been slow, and the expense of maintaining a home for his new daughter had been high.

When Chloe's doctor had told him she must be removed to a more healthful climate if she was to survive another summer Oliver's bank account had been flat. To pay the cost of his daughter's summer in Arizona he'd borrowed money from William Pinkerton. Were it not for this obligation William would not have been able to persuade him to take on this cursed Aballo case.

Oliver folded Chloe's letter and stared out at the water. The child felt displaced in Arizona. And no wonder, he thought. Chloe had barely had time to adjust to living with a brand new father in Baltimore. Now, once again, she was dragged from her home and dropped all alone in a strange country with only Mrs. Milawney for a companion.

Surely it was better for Chloe to be in a place where she could breathe free. Oliver sighed. He'd hoped that by now his child would have made a friend on the ranch. Obviously, that hadn't happened. Even in Baltimore Jimmy was really Chloe's only playmate.

It wasn't that she never came into contact with other children. Oliver had scratched up enough money to allow her to attend a private day school for young ladies. But she had made no close friends at the school. This was partly due to her shyness. But he acknowledged that it was equally due to his own reticence.

He had avoided a more than passing acquaintance with the school's other parents because he didn't want them to know that Chloe's mother had been an unmarried actress. He feared his child might be scorned if that were common knowledge. What would happen if Marietta flaunted herself in Baltimore? Was she actress enough to behave like a respectable woman when she visited Chloe?

Frowning, he tucked the little paper into his breast pocket and then opened his housekeeper's letter.

Dear Sir, It's well I'm hoping you are. We miss Baltimore and look forward to coming home in the fall when the weather isn't hotter than a frying pan on a bonfire. The air here is wonderful clean and the mountains are a sight for sore eyes. Chloe's breathing like a lamb in a meadow and sleeping sound as a doorstop. As you know, sleeping don't come easy to the mite. It's a relief to me not to have to boil up all those kettles of water for her to breathe in the steam. As for the company, Mrs. MacGill, the rancher's wife, seems a good enough sort of woman. The cowboys are a rough lot but leave us alone. Yestiday I had words with that worthless Mr. Schurman who cooks for the bunkhouse. He left us a can of sour milk. I gave him a good tongue-lashing! He promises it won't happen again. Y'r humble servant, Edith T. Milawney

Oliver folded the second letter. Across the park a boat with a red sail glided into the harbor. His gaze followed it but the image before his mind's eye was of Chloe struggling for air on a sweltering summer night in the city.

She had her mother's auburn hair and pretty face but not her robust health and resilient personality. He rubbed his forehead. Was he making a terrible mistake considering letting Marietta back into Chloe's life?

"Ho, Redcastle!"

John Brown Junior and Emil Venator were heading in his direction. He stood and waited until they crossed the park and stopped in front of him.

Brown shook his hand as if he were a dear old friend. "I'm glad to see you survived our ordeal!"

"And I you. How did you manage to make it to shore?"

Brown said, "I've surveyed this lake. If I do say so myself, I know the area around the islands like the back of my hand. Fortunately we were thrown out of the boat near a shallow spot."

Venator interrupted, "Never would I have found it! The waves, they were over my head!" He whirled his arms. "Brown grabbed my hand and dragged me to safety. Let me tell you, this man is my savior!"

John Brown Junior shrugged. "We simply waited until the winds died down and then walked to shore. What about you?"

"I had a bad night, but not as bad as the one Gabriel Goggins had."

All three men sobered as they considered Gabriel's fate. Venator said, "I hear his boat was recovered near the Ballast island.

"Is that so?"

"Ironic is it not--considering Ballast would have been his ultimate destination if he hadn't been lost in the storm. Somehow his boat found its way home."

The men exchanged a few more words and then Brown repeated his invitation to go caving. "We are nearly finished with our job in the caves, but there's still an afternoon's worth of work left to do. You might find it interesting."

Oliver accepted and they agreed to meet the next day. Alone again, he resumed his seat on the bench. The crunch of paper inside his coat pocket reminded him that he hadn't read William Pinkerton's telegram. Absent mindedly he unfolded it.

"Clerk in law office of Wald and Charlevoix says GG leaves fortune to HM. G lawyer member of ACA, presently attending meet in the islands. Seek out."

CHAPTER THIRTEEN

Oliver left the park and headed toward one of the many narrow wooden docks forking the harbor.

The day had turned sultry. He dodged sweating fishermen racing to unload their catch. A sailor shook his fist at seabirds screeching over a boatload of wriggling perch. On nearby Doller's dock disembarking ferry passengers added to the confusion.

Oliver stopped a brawny young man in overalls. "I'm looking to hire someone to take me over to Ballast Island. Can you help me."

"Not today. Got business to tend. Feller over there might be willing." He pointed at a weather-beaten catboat tied up at the next dock.

Oliver squinted at the disheveled individual sprawled unconscious in its cockpit. A few minutes later he gave the catboat's mast a kick that shook Gene Waterman awake.

"Hey! What the. . ." Waterman peered up with bloodshot eyes. "Thought you was drowned."

"Sorry to disappoint you. Gabriel Goggins died in last night's storm."

"Heard that."

"You don't sound heartbroken."

Waterman shrugged. "Young fool, thinking he could out-sail one of our Erie blows. Got what he deserved, if you ask me. What you doing here?"

"Saving your skin. Do you make a habit of sleeping in public?" Oliver cast a disapproving eye over Waterman's seedy bulk. He hadn't changed clothes since the banquet. Food stains splotched his creased shirtfront. His wrinkled trousers were torn at the knee.

"You wasn't the only one caught in a storm. Between serving up slop to that horde of fancy folk and barely making it back here in one piece I had a helluva night. Must have dozed off."

"You were sleeping with your face full in the sun. Another hour and you'd be sizzling like bacon on a campfire."

Grunting, Waterman pushed himself into a sitting position. "Hat fell off." He rummaged, finally locating a wide-brimmed straw and cramming it onto his bald head. "You wake me up to ruin my afternoon or you here for a reason?"

"I want transportation to Ballast Island. Is this boat capable of making the trip?"

"Pretty Girl's capable. That don't mean she's leaving the dock today. Her toe rail got banged up in last night's blow, and I need my beauty sleep."

"You need to earn your pay.'

"That right? Well, first I need to see it."

"I already gave you an advance on work you haven't done yet. Move over." Oliver started to swing himself onto the sailboat's deck."

Waterman grabbed his leg and pushed back. "Hold your horses! What makes you think you can order me around? This is my boat and I ain't your servant!"

Oliver reached into his pocket and withdrew a bill. "Will this pay my way?"

Waterman stared at it, then licked his lips. "I ain't had nothin' to eat. We need provisions!"

"Fine. Let's go shopping."

It was more than an hour before they were able to leave the dock, and quite a bit longer before they cleared the harbor. As they drifted past Gibralter the catboat's huge canvas sail flapped in the faint breeze.

Waterman said, "Wind always dies this time of day. Airs light as this we won't make Ballast 'til dinner time."

"That will have to be good enough."

"Ain't good enough for me being out in this sun. I already got a burn."

"Whose fault is that?"

"Dammit, Redcastle, your lack of consideration ain't hardly human. Why are you in such a tear to get to Ballast?"

"Goggins' boat washed up over there."

"So?"

"I want to take a look at it."

"What you think that boat can tell you?"

"Won't know until I see it. I think the wind just freshened. Pull that sail in."

Hot and irritable, they neared their destination just after six o'clock. As their shabby vessel, the misnamed "Pretty Girl," drifted into a shallow bay, two sleek sailing canoes coasted past them. Their captains and crews waved. Oliver waved back. Waterman pretended not to see.

Visible in the distance other vessels lay on a rocky beach where their owners worked at polish and repair. Sails and lines on the limestone shore spread drying in the last rays of sun.

Once Pretty Girl was anchored, Oliver and Waterman waded ashore. A nattily dressed young man lounging under a tree with a pair of attractive young ladies greeted them.

"Ho there! Welcome to our island paradise! You here for tonight's race?"

Oliver explained that he'd come to take a look at Gabriel Goggins wrecked boat. The young man scrambled to his feet and led them past a clump of scrubby trees to the broken remains of Magic Carpet.

"Sad sight," the young man muttered. "We found her this morning drifting fifty yards from the island, almost as if she was trying to find her way home."

Waterman snorted at this fanciful notion and parked himself on a rock. Oliver walked toward the wreck. The top half of Goggins' mast was missing. A few shreds of mainsail clung to the shattered boom. He pictured Gabriel as he'd last seen him, white-faced, clinging to the tiller. Had he simply been washed overboard? Was damage to the boat due to the storm, or something more?

As he crouched over the ruin a stout white-haired man came up. "Name's Clement, Wendell C. Clement. I'm the club's secretary. What can I do for you?"

Oliver introduced himself and Waterman and then pointed at the stump which had once been Magic Carpet's mast. "What could have caused a stout piece of wood like that to break off so clean?"

Clement shook his head. "Damned if I know. Goggins wasn't much of a sailor, but Magic Carpet was built to weather Erie storms."

Oliver rubbed the mast'e broken edge. "This feels smooth, almost as if it was partially cut with a saw instead of snapped off by wind. Are you sure the mast was sound? A piece of wood can look good on the outside and be rotten within."

"Do you see rot?"

"No. It looks clean."

"Talk to the man who built her. Goggins bought Magic Carpet from Jacob Alister, the finest builder of racing canoes in this part of the world. He's under yon cottonwood." Clement indicated a tent set in the shade on the hill above them. "Meanwhile," he added, "you and your friend are welcome to join our mess. Nothing fancy, but plenty of good wholesome food and fellowship."

After Clement walked off Oliver returned to Waterman. "You heard him. Want to go with me to talk to Alister or would you rather get some dinner?"

"I 'spose you intend jawing with the swells here until nightfall." Waterman's expression was sullen.

"Most likely."

"What choice have I got then? Ain't I your slave for the day?"

"You've been hired for a job if that's what you mean."

"You got your point of view and I got mine. I'll go fill my belly."

Waterman stumbled toward the clubhouse, and Oliver made his way up an incline toward a grassy plateau.

The island was beautiful but tiny. He guessed it to be no more than a few square acres. A log cabin had been constructed on a slight hill with a commanding view of the lake and the Bass islands. Tents clustered near the dock and surrounding trees, many fitted out with brilliantly colored Turkey rugs and comfortable looking chairs.

Oliver found Alister sitting in front of his tent with two other men. He was a small, spry looking man with a thick head of dark brown hair and bushy gray eyebrows. He seemed glad to talk about Magic Carpet.

"Perhaps you'll not understand this," he said, "but finding her all smashed up this morning was almost like discovering one of my own children broken to bits." He shook his head. "I built every inch of her. She was a real beauty and now look what's happened."

"You should never have sold her to Gabriel," said one of his companions. "Poor booby couldn't sail his way through a mud puddle. In all the time he raced with the club he never came in anything but dead last."

"Oh not so!" another man chimed in. "I remember distinctly once he came in next to last. That was when Ridgely got so drunk he rounded the mark in the wrong direction." The group laughed heartily at this, then sobered, remembering that the butt of their joke was now dead.

Alister said, "Gabriel offered me a price I couldn't turn down. I knew he'd disgrace Magic Carpet in the races but how could I know it would end like this?"

After talking to the three men for another twenty minutes Oliver had picked up a sad picture of Gabriel's standing with the canoe racers. He had been the organization's unwitting buffoon, enthusiastic but incompetent at everything he tried.

Seemingly, they had tolerated him only because of his good nature and huge fortune. Perhaps that explained his devotion to the Mussmans. Vulnerable and alone, having just lost his father, his only real family, Gabriel must have been desperate for acceptance. The Mussmans had provided him with that.

Thoughtfully, Oliver made his way to the clubhouse. Over a meal of roasted tomatoes, steak, chicken, bread and a variety of stewed and fresh fruits, he talked to Gabriel's lawyer, a balding, pot-bellied man named Harold Wald.

At first Wald was circumspect, refusing to answer many of Oliver's questions. But after he'd cleaned his overflowing dinner plate and downed several tankards of dark ale, he grew loquacious.

"Gabriel's father and I grew up attending the same church. We were friends from boyhood. It was a black day for me when Samuel Goggins died, but perhaps it's as well he never lived to see what's just happened."

"It must have been hard on Gabriel to lose his only remaining parent so early in life."

"Devastating. Gabriel never had the sense of a May fly but Sam kept him on the straight and narrow. They were complete opposites."

"Gabriel and his father?"

"Oh my, yes! First and last, Sam Goggins was a hard-headed businessman. He'd roll over in his grave to know what Gabriel was doing to his business."

"What was that?"

"Ruining it. Gabriel had no more idea how to run a hardware business than my cat. Then there was this nonsense with the Mussmans."

"You refer to Leander Mussman's religious sect."

"I refer to the whole piece of foolishness. Gabriel was completely taken in by Mussman." Wald slammed his tankard down indignantly. "Then when the man dangled his pretty daughter in front of the boy he simply lost what little sense was left to him. I argued until I was blue in the face but I couldn't stop him."

"Stop him from doing what?"

"From signing away his entire fortune to that passel of charlatans."

"You mean Gabriel left all his inheritance to Leander Mussman?"

"Gabriel left it all to the daughter. Hermione Mussman gets it all."

"Hermione is still a teenager."

"According to the provisions of the will, her father is to manage the money until her twenty-first birthday."

"Leander Mussman is not a well man. What if he never regains consciousness?"

"Then his legal spouse will take control."

CHAPTER FOURTEEN

"If we'd got off Ballast before sunset we wouldn't be stuck out here." Waterman jerked Pretty Girl's limp sail. It sagged back uselessly.

Oliver eased his shoulder against the boat's mast and stretched one of his long legs. He gazed over the quiet lake. Stars glimmered in its onyx surface like tiny reflected diamonds. The air felt soft against his cheek, like a woman's warm breath. "I don't see a problem."

Waterman snorted. "That's a hot one. You see problems everywhere you set foot. Why'd you have to spend so long jabbering to them swells on Ballast? What's it to you that Gabriel Goggins fell of his boat and drowned himself?"

"Maybe he didn't fall. Maybe he was pushed."

Waterman shook the drooping sail again. "That's crazy talk."

"Goggins lawyer tells me he left his fortune to Hermione Mussman."

Waterman whistled. "You think the girl had something to do with Goggins drowning?"

"Not the girl herself. It's possible her bandit lover might have been involved. She was with him on Middle Bass that night."

"I didn't see him."

"You don't seem to see much that's useful to this investigation."

"We're back to that? You think I'm not earning my pay?" Waterman hurled an empty box at Oliver's head. He dodged, and it skipped over the boat's side rail and splashed into the still water.

"Do that again and I'll throw you overboard."

"Then what?" Waterman sneered. "You ain't no sailor. You plan to swim home? We're in the middle of Lake Erie and looks like we'll be here half the night. I got you at my mercy, Redcastle."

"What's eating you?" Oliver asked curiously. "Why are you so surly? I remember you as quite a friendly fellow."

"The years can change a man."

"They certainly changed you." Oliver pictured the spry, cheerful, ambitious young man Gene Rucker had been as a new recruit to the Pinkertons. He shook his head. "Ever since we met up you've been like a porcupine sitting on a nest of hornets. William Pinkerton is paying you good money. If you don't want this job say so."

"You're no different from him and his greedy, hardhearted pa. You think money will buy anything or anybody. Well some things money ain't good for!"

"What are you talking about?"

Waterman turned his face away. "Nothing that would interest a big war hero like you," he said sullenly.

"I wasn't a hero, and the war's been over since nigh on twenty years. Something about it still sticks in your craw? Spit it out. What's Pinkertons done to you?"

"None of your damn business."

"Your sorry attitude is making it my business. There's a reason why you quit the agency, why you've been hiding out on this island all these years, why you've turned into a no account sot."

"No account sot, am I?" Waterman sputtered with rage. "Well maybe that's what I am. You'd be the same if you'd gone through what I did."

"And what was that?"

"Look here, you know about the Ohio prison camps?"

"Everybody's heard about Johnson Island."

"Camp Chase was just as bad, maybe worse. Three thousand prisoners bottled up at Chase in 1863. Conditions straight out of your worst nightmare."

Oliver nodded. Southern prisons had been hell-holes as much out of necessity as malice. By the end of the war the southerners had been too poor to feed themselves much less their prisoners. Northerners, on the other hand, after hearing about conditions in the south, had mistreated their Confederate prisoners out of sheer spite.

He said, "Anyone with a drop of humanity would feel sorry for the poor devils stuck in Johnsons and Chase. But that was a long time ago."

"Not if you was one of them. A man who spent time in Chase is branded for life. How could he forget what he went through when he can't close his eyes without having night sweats about the place?"

"You're saying you were captive there?"

"I wasn't a real prisoner. I was a spy."

"You spied for Pinkertons at Camp Chase?"

"Young fool that I was! You're right about me being different when I was young. I was spunky, adventurous, ready to volunteer for anything that I thought might get me a leg up in this world."

"You volunteered to spy at Chase?"

"It started when that Reb General, Morgan, escaped the Ohio Penitentiary by tunneling through four feet of stone and twenty feet of dirt. The bosses figured if they couldn't hold Morgan others might escape from Camp Chase."

"Why not?"

"Some did. So they hired private detectives and lured bona fide prisoners to spy on comrades. I was one of the detectives. Other prisoners caught onto us soon enough. Razorbacks they called us."

"What happened?

Waterman sat silent for a moment, his shoulders hunched and his face buried in shadow. Finally, he said, "They came for me in the dead of night. I woke up with hands around my throat. They took me from my bunk, blanket wrapped around my head to stifle my screams. I'll never forget the stink of that blanket. Makes me gag thinking of it."

"What did they do to you?"

"Kicked and beat on me. Whispered their curses cause they didn't want nobody to hear. Finally, they pushed me head first into a barrel of water that stood at a corner of the barracks. I can still remember how it felt, thrashing and choking, their hands holding me down." He shuddered. "I would have drowned only one of the guards finally heard the ruckus and got me out before I was dead."

"You were lucky."

"Yeah, lucky. Me just a kid and my life ruined before it even stated."

"Why ruined? You made it out alive."

"Half alive, more like. From then on I was a marked man. More than a hundred Reb prisoners knowing me for a Razorback and vowing to see me dead soon as they got the chance."

"How many of those men got out of Chase alive?"

"Enough."

"You mean they're still after you?"

"Some things never get forgotten. You know that, Redcastle. You made plenty of enemies working for Pinkertons. Any of them come after you?"

"It's happened."

"What did you do about it?"

"Dealt with it."

"That's all you're going to say, I suppose."

"No reason to say more."

"You sleep sound at night?"

"Sound enough."

"That's a damned lie! When a man feels his enemies hunting him like a pack of damned wolves he don't sleep sound."

Oliver cocked his head. "Now I understand. You changed your name and came to these islands for the same reason as the Browns—to escape your enemies."

"Leastways, if they come at me on Put-In-Bay I got a fighting chance."

"It's been near twenty years. Some of the Rebs that got out of Chase are dead by now. Others have gone back south and settled with wives and children. They've put the past behind them."

"You telling me you don't look over your shoulder from time to time?"

"A man can't spend his life hiding in a corner. You're jumping at shadows for no reason. Even if one of your old foes were to step off a ferry the two of you wouldn't recognize each other."

"I recognized you, Redcastle. Knew you were Pinkerton's golden boy the minute I saw you. Allan Pinkerton thought high of you but he didn't have the same regard for me. He squashed my life like I was no more than a bug on his carpet."

A cool wind rippled across the water and the sail filled. Pretty girl jumped forward as if someone had given her flanks a whack.

Waterman said, "Looks like we'll make it home tonight after all. Ain't we lucky."

CHAPTER FIFTEEN

A brisk night wind pushed Pretty Girl's bow into the dock. Oliver climbed out of the boat and remarked, "It's not so late. More than an hour to midnight by the look of the moon."

Waterman looped a line over a weathered piling. "Past my bedtime. Thanks to you I haven't had a decent night's sleep since two days. Here, get your paws off that line. I know how to take care of my boat. You go about your business and good riddance."

"Fine. Sweet dreams." Happy to leave his cohort to his own bad-tempered company, Oliver sauntered off. Since revealing the humiliations of his past Waterman had been as pleasant a companion as a cornered wolf spider. Collaboration with him had confirmed Oliver's conviction that it was better to work solo.

Despite the late hour Put-In-Bay was lively. Across the park ladies in gauzy summer dresses paraded down Delaware Avenue. Alongside them men in shirtsleeves held onto straw hats threatened by the stiff breeze that had come up so suddenly.

Oliver stopped short, his progress across the track fronting the harbor cut off by a solitary horse. It pulled a dilapidated cart filled with a half dozen young boys shouting good-natured insults at one another.

Nearby, children played a game of Blind man's Buff around the fountain. Their whoops of laughter seemed muffled by the moonlit darkness, caught in the fluttering net of wind-laced branches overhead. Oliver had to jump off the path bisecting the park to avoid a pair of urchins in hot pursuit of one another.

"Ho there, Redcastle, where've you been? I was just inquiring for you at your hotel."

Owen and John Brown stood under a gas lamp. A cloud of insects attracted by the light fluttered around their heads.

Oliver explained that he had been to Ballast to have a look at Gabriel Goggins' boat.

John observed, "How pleasant that banquet at Middle Bass seemed while we were enjoying it. What a terrible conclusion to a happy occasion."

Oliver nodded. "Terrible indeed. What news of Leander Mussman? Has he regained consciousness?"

Owen shook his head. "Still dead to the world."

John said, "We may have to brace ourselves for more bad news."

"What does your guest think of all this?" Oliver asked.

"Emil?" John rolled his eyes. "The man's had a more harrowing visit than either of us anticipated. Fortunately, he's a hardy soul and here to do business. Last night's events haven't changed that. I hope you still plan to join us for caving."

"I'm looking forward to it. Will Owen be in the party?"

Owen put up a hand. "Never cared much for caves. I'm an open-air man. Speaking of which, it's time I got myself home to Gibralter."

John asked his brother, "Where do you sleep now that Mussman and his womenfolk have taken over your cottage?"

"I've fixed up a place in the shed back of Cooke's garden. It'll do 'til they leave."

"That could be a long time. Mussman's brain sickness might linger for months. If you get tired of sleeping rough you're welcome to stay with us. We'd enjoy the company."

Owen hunched his shoulders. "I'm fine where I am. Lord knows I've spent plenty of nights with only the trees for shelter. We both have, isn't that right brother?"

John acknowledged the truth of that observation with a wry smile. A few minutes later the brothers parted. Oliver accompanied Owen up the shore road to the spot in Squaw Harbor where he'd left his rowboat.

In the moonlight Gibralter's round hump resembled a turtle in a bathtub. Oliver commented that Cooke's little island looked close enough to spit at.

"You could almost walk it from here," Owen agreed. "There's a bar sticking out from Gibralter nearly to this point. Most of it's hardly more than a foot below water this time of year. Boaters who don't know that often go aground. I've sat on my porch and watched half a dozen fancy boats come to grief on it all in one afternoon." He chuckled at the memory.

"That's a sweet little cottage you've got. It's good of you to let Mussman's family take it over."

"Nothing for it. Couldn't move that preacher's wife out of my bedroom if I wanted to. Poor woman is beside herself. When she isn't on her knees praying for her man's recovery, she's pacing the floor like a caged squirrel."

"What of the daughter?"

"Mighty pretty girl. She makes a picture standing on the cliff outside the cottage. Stays there by the hour staring at the water like she wished she could grow wings and fly." Owen shook his head. "Can't be pleasant, cooped up with a stepmother half crazed by worry and a father who's lying on a stranger's bed with no more sign of life in him than a brick."

Oliver agreed that this was a sad state of affairs. He helped Owen push his boat off the shale and watched him row back to Gibralter with strong, steady sweeps of his oars. There was strength in his arms. Though he was fighting the wind the trip took no more than ten minutes.

After he'd disappeared Oliver found a ledge and sat down. It was a beautiful evening. The moon and stars struck silver paths on the water. Birds twittered in the trees. In the distance he heard laughter and someone singing. The singing was followed by applause. He supposed he must be hearing the tail end of Marietta's Shakespearian performance.

He had been sitting quietly perhaps a quarter of an hour when an unusual motion on the water caught his eye. A rowboat slipped out from the shadows along Gibralter's shoreline. It wobbled uncertainly and then headed in fits and starts toward Peach Point. The person directing it could not be Owen Brown. Brown would not row with so little authority. The oarsman's shape didn't look like Brown's either. In fact, it looked like a woman.

Oliver stared. Then, as he recognized the figure of Hermione Mussman, he set off on a run along the dirt track, hoping to catch her before the wind blew her into shore.

The road hooked right just where a thick stand of trees hid her progress from view. As Oliver trotted past them the moon slipped behind a wisp of cloud plunging the road into deep darkness. He stopped, trying to get his bearings. Gradually his eyes adjusted and he began picking his way through the trees and back toward the water. He saw no sign of Hermione and suspected he was too late to intercept her. She'd had time to beach her boat along the shoreline at any number of spots.

The laughter and singing he'd heard earlier were much louder. In the distance to his left applause and shouts of "Huzzah!" broke out. This must be where The Elysian Players were staging their production of Midsummer Night's Dream. Could that be where Hermione was heading? He remembered that she'd expressed a desire to see the play. But why had she come to it when the performance was ending?

Perhaps Hermione hadn't been able to get away from Agatha until now. Or possibly it wasn't the play that interested her. Perhaps she had an assignation.

Hoping to learn more, he prowled along the water's edge. In the dark this was no easy task. Lurching over rocks and bushes, he almost fell over a rowboat abandoned on the pebbled beach.

He knelt to touch the boat's dripping oar. Now he knew for sure that Hermione had made it to shore before he could intercept her. He heard a splash and lifted his head. Picked out by the moonlight some twenty yards off he saw a figure drop an anchor and then climb awkwardly out of what appeared to be a canoe. Hoisting long skirts above her knees and muttering complaints into the wind the figure waded onto the rocky beach. Oliver recognized Agatha Mussman.

Oliver asked himself if he'd mistaken Agatha for Hermione. But no, he was certain the person he'd seen rowing earlier had been Mussman's shapely young daughter. She had come in the wet boat at his feet. Apparently Agatha had followed her.

As she stumbled up from the beach in her sodden clothing Agatha made so much racket that Oliver was easily able to trail behind her without being detected. She headed directly toward the laughter and applause still being carried on the wind.

The Elysian Players had selected a grassy site with a view of the lake for their outdoor production. Two tents had been set up for the actors' convenience. The lantern-lit stage was an open pavilion in front of the tents. The audience had seated itself on blankets and folding camp chairs.

Now that the performance was ended they mingled with the actors in chattering knots. Oliver caught sight of Marietta at the center of a group of admiring men. She was got up as the fairy queen Titania, her filmy costume stopping well above her knees and barely covering her breasts. Except for daisy-chain anklets her feet were bare. Flowers woven into a crown sat atop her thick red hair which hung loose over her bare shoulders. Another actress dressed as a wood sprite stood next to her. Though she, too, was a fetchingly costumed, Marietta's sensual beauty drew all eyes, including Agatha's. She headed directly for her.

Oliver dragged his gaze away and scanned the crowd. After several minutes he saw the back of a young girl who might be Hermione. She disappeared behind a tree. He followed but when he arrived at the spot there was no sign of her. He searched the area but couldn't find the girl.

Frustrated, he emerged from the trees and returned his attention to the people clustering around Marietta.

Marietta's male admirers had dropped back. She, Agatha and the other actress were having a noisy confrontation. Marietta gave Agatha a shove that sent her stumbling backward. As she fell onto the grass Marietta and her acting colleague scampered across the grass toward a tent.

Two men helped Agatha to her feet. The moment she was upright she brushed them off and pursued Marietta. But she had disappeared into the tent. A sturdy young man, clad as one of the bumpkins in the play, planted himself in the entrance and barred Agatha's way. After exchanging several heated words with him, Agatha turned on her heel. As she headed back the way she had come her face was a study in rage.

Oliver watched this scene in amazement. He had assumed that Mussman's wife had rowed from Gibralter in pursuit of Hermione. But she hadn't even looked for the girl and didn't seem to be aware that her stepdaughter had flown the coop. What was going on between Agatha and Marietta, he wondered. Surely Agatha would have no cause for jealousy when her husband had been unconscious since the previous night.

He followed Agatha across the track and back to the shoreline. If she had turned to look back she would have seen him. But she was too caught up in her private emotional turmoil to notice that she was not alone.

He stood under a tree and watched as she climbed into her canoe, nearly tipping herself into the water. Finally, she managed to settle herself in the vessel and head back to Gibralter.

At a loss, Oliver watched her slow progress toward Jay Cooke's island. Below him he could see Hermione's boat. Where was she? A moment later the question was answered. Hermione stepped out of the shadows and sat down on a rock. When Agatha had disappeared from sight she covered her face with her hands. Oliver heard the sound of weeping.

CHAPTER SIXTEEN

Blinded by her tears, Hermione didn't notice Oliver approach until he stood within two feet of her. When finally she perceived him she screeched.

He put a firm hand on her shoulder. "You've nothing to fear from me. No, don't try pulling away. I'm not letting go until you answer some questions."

"What do you want? Why are you spying on me?" She stared up at him, twisting a crumpled handkerchief between her hands. Moonlight glistened on her tear-streaked face.

He asked, "What are you doing here at this hour? Are you hiding from your stepmother?"

"I'm not."

"You are."

She looked away. "I came to see the play."

"So late? The play was over when you got here. You rowed from Gibralter for another reason. You came to meet someone."

"If that's true, where is he?"

"He? You mean Frank Aballo. Yes, where is he?"

She struggled to control her trembling lips, then covered her face again. "Go away! Leave me alone!"

As he listened to her loud weeping Oliver softened his grip on her shoulder. "What's the trouble Hermione?"

"What do you care?"

"If I can I'll help you."

"Nobody can help me!" she wailed. Frank was supposed to meet me here. Something's wrong. I know it!"

"He didn't show?"

"No, no! And that's not like him! He always keeps his word!"

Had she not been so distressed Oliver would have been amused by her faith in a bank-robber's constancy. He asked, "When was the last time you saw him?"

"Oh you know very well! It was that horrible night at Middle Bass."

"Last night before Gabriel Goggins was drowned and your father injured?"

"You know it. You saw us together. So many terrible things have happened that it seems years ago. I can hardly believe it was only last night."

"And that was where you agreed to meet him again here?"

"Yes, yes! Why are you questioning me like this?" She stared at Oliver. "Are you a policeman?"

"I'm a detective working privately for a train company."

"Train company? You mean. . ."

"Yes, I'm working for the train company Frank Aballo robbed."

Hermione burst into fresh tears. "I suppose you want to put him in jail. Oh please don't do that! Frank isn't a bad person!"

"He's a thief."

"Only because he's been mistreated. He was reformed. We prayed together every day. He would never have robbed that train if Daddy hadn't thrown him out of the congregation."

"He stole a payroll belonging to a lot of people. The people I work for want that money back."

"I've told Frank he must return all of it. He will. I know he will. If we're to marry we must start fresh and without sin. Besides, we don't need. . ."

When she didn't finish the sentence Oliver finished it for her. "Now that Gabriel Goggins is dead and you've inherited his fortune you and Frank don't need ill-gotten gains."

Again Hermione dissolved into tears. "I didn't want any of this to happen. You must believe me. I didn't want Gabriel to die! I only wanted him to go away. Now he's dead and I don't know what's happened to Frank. It's all so awful!"

Hermione resumed sobbing wildly. Since she was obviously in no condition to row herself back to Gibralter Oliver decided to take her himself. Lifting her by the elbows he helped her stumble across the rocks and into her boat. When she was settled he pushed off and climbed in himself. While he rowed she huddled in the stern with her head down and her arms wrapped around her chest.

When her crying finally subsided he asked, "What will Agatha say when you get back?"

Hermione moaned. "I can't talk to her. I can't!"

"She is your stepmother, after all."

"Not because I desired the relationsip. My father should never have married her. She threw herself at him. She pursued him until he finally gave in."

"I gather you and your stepmother don't get along?"

"If it weren't for her Frank and I would be together now and he would never have robbed that train. It was she who arranged the engagement with Gabriel." Hermione added venomously, "Everything that's happened is her doing! All of it!"

Oliver doubted that this was true. If Agatha had scotched the romance between Hermione and Aballo she'd had good reason. It wasn't her fault that Hermione's lover had a penchant for robbery. Moreover, it couldn't be Agatha's fault that Leander had nearly drowned in a sudden storm on Lake Erie.

Oliver asked, "How will you get into Owen Brown's cottage without waking Agatha?"

"The same way I got out."

"Through a window?"

Hermione nodded and Oliver wondered if the girl would be able to return to her bed without a confrontation. If Agatha caught them together what would she have to say? And what would he have to say to Agatha?

Fortunately, this unhappy eventuality did not occur. Hermione slipped quietly into the window she had left open. Oliver stood outside a good quarter of an hour but heard no disturbance inside the dark cottage. Finally, he turned away.

Instead of heading back to the boat, he climbed up the path and across the lawn in front of Cooke's mansion to the a spot which commanded a magnificent view of the lake. He wanted to enjoy a quiet moment looking at the islands. But when he arrived he found the place already occupied.

Oliver started to back away but the man seated in a wicker chair croaked, "Who goes there?"

"General Grant, sir, I'm sorry to intrude."

Grant was hatless and wore a loose canvas jacket. The moonlight picked out his short white beard and the dark wells of his eyes. Though his body appeared shrunken his rugged features were still handsome. He said mildly, "I'm pleased you didn't call me President Grant. I was very glad to relinquish that title."

"Oh Indeed, sir. I apologize again. Force of habit."

"You're a soldier then?"

"Yes, sir."

"Union?"

"Yes, sir."

"You didn't give me your name."

"Oliver Redcastle, Sir."

"Redcastle, Redcastle. Sounds familiar. I've heard that name before. Who did you serve under?"

"General McClellan, sir. I was a sharpshooter."

"Ah, that's why I recognize the name. You had quite a reputation. Served Little Mac well." He was silent a moment. "His men loved him."

"They did."

"And he loved them. That was his weakness. I've been thinking a good deal about weakness lately. A general must send good men to their deaths. Little Mac hated that part of the job so much he drew back when he should have gritted his teeth and plunged in."

"So they say."

Grant shrugged. "Oh well, don't suppose it matters now. There's no bringing back the dead. Why are you here at this hour, Redcastle? Didn't come to have a depressing conversation with me, I'll wager." Grant's voice was hoarse. Clearly, he found it difficult to speak.

"No, Sir, though any conversation with you is an honor."

"There are those who wouldn't say so."

"I'm not among them. I know what you accomplished. I was at Vicksburg. You were a fighter."

"Bloody Vicksburg."

"Bloody, but it was the turning."

"Perhaps." Grant shook his head. "I consigned fine young men to their graves at that place—fine young men on both sides. A man thinks of that when he reaches my age and condition. I was thinking of it when you approached—of human frailty, particularly my own. Perhaps that's why I said what I did of poor McClellan."

"It was a brutal war. There was no fighting it without death. It couldn't be helped."

"No, of course it couldn't. Sometimes I wonder if anything can be helped. Mark my words, one day you'll look back on your life and wonder the same." His humorless chuckle turned into a series of harsh coughs.

Oliver said, "You could be right."

"I am right. When it happens, remember this conversation."

"I'll do that, Sir."

"Then you'll be doing me a service. I'm not long for this world, Mr. Redcastle. I'm writing a book but who knows if anyone will read the damned thing. Think of me now and then."

"You may be sure that I will."

"Good night to you Mr. Redcastle."

"Good night, Sir."

CHAPTER SEVENTEEN

Back on Put In Bay Oliver found the village streets were quiet and most houses dark. Three lights shone in the upstairs windows of the Beebe House. He stared up. One of those lighted windows was his. Somebody was moving around inside his room.

He hurried into the hotel and up the staircase. Hearing stealthy movements on the other side of his closed door, he yanked it open and tackled the intruder. Marietta and the bedsprings squealed as they landed in a tangle of legs and silky skirts.

"Stop it! Get off me!"

"Gladly." Her warm uncorseted body molded itself to his, and her perfume invaded his nostrils. Extricating himself, he asked roughly, "What the hell are you doing pilfering my room?"

"I wasn't pilfering!" She raised herself off the bed. He saw that she wore a lace negligee that exposed the tops of her breasts. After making a show of smoothing the gauzy garment's ruffled folds around her hips she took several cautious steps around him.

He glared at her. "Half the bureau drawers are hanging open. You've been going through my things."

"So what if I have? You've gone through mine often enough." She raised an eyebrow, emphasizing the double entendre.

"What's that?" He pointed at a folded paper peeking out from her plump décolletage.

She put up a protective hand. "None of your business."

"It's mine!"

"No!" She whirled and ran out through the open door. Considering the encumbrance of her diaphanous clothing she raced down the hall with surprising speed. Oliver didn't catch up with her until she had flung open her own door and was halfway through it.

He pushed her inside the room and slammed the door closed. When she tried to evade his grasp, he tackled her. Once again they wound up on the bed. A single candle burned on the bedside table. In its flickering light he plucked the piece of paper from between her breasts. It was Chloe's note.

She spat out, "Brute! You think you can make free with me because you're a man."

"You were making free with my room and my belongings."

"Only to discover what you'd done with my baby. When I saw you sneak off to Gibralter with Hermione Mussman I seized my opportunity."

"To spy!"

"To turn the tables! What were you up to with that preacher's daughter? You're old enough to be her father, Oliver."

"Only if I'd sired her in my teens."

"Pshaw!"

"How did you happen to see me with Hermione?"

She relaxed under him and lay back against her pillow. "You're not invisible. I saw you lurking around the actor's tent after the performance. I followed you. Why not? I thought perhaps you'd come to see me?"

"You were wrong. I wasn't there to see you."

Her expression soured. "So you admit you were chasing after Hermione?"

"My interest in the girl is professional. I'm commissioned to catch her train robber lover."

"By substituting yourself in her affections! You carried that child into the boat as if she were a china doll in need of your special mending. I know a man making up to a female when I see it."

"As you certainly should, given all your experience!"

"You like nothing better than to insult me!"

"You're trying to change the subject. It won't work. I want to know what you were up to in my room."

"My concern is what you're up to. Why have you shuttled Chloe off to Arizona?"

"So, it's what I thought. You've gone through all my private correspondence." He searched his memory. Had Mrs. Milawney's letter contained any specifics about the location of the ranch where she and Chloe were staying? He thought not.

"I have every right to know what you've done with my daughter."

Marietta lay completely relaxed now. Idly, she twirled one of her curls around her finger. Her wide green eyes gazed up at him and her lips parted. The candlelight diffused a golden radiance that made her flawless skin seem to glow. He found himself thinking that she could have been the model for an Italian painting of an angel.

Inwardly, he scoffed at that notion, telling himself that Marietta Dumont was no angel.

He said gruffly, "You needn't be concerned about Chloe. She's in a safe place, a place where she can breathe free. Baltimore summers are not good for her health."

"She still suffers from the asthma?"

"Very much."

Marietta lowered her eyelids and sighed. "She gets it from my side of the family. My mother was crippled by the breathing difficulty."

"She was?"

"Oh, indeed! I suspect that's why my father left us. The poor woman was always sick."

"Your father abandoned you?"

"When I was twelve. How did you think I became an actress?"

"I never thought about it."

"Of course you didn't. You wanted my body not my history."

It was true. He couldn't deny it.

She laughed wryly. "Most women don't take up the stage in the normal course of things. What sane woman enjoys being a social outcast?"

"I thought you liked the life."

"I do but I'm not a complete fool. Even at that young age I knew very well that going on the stage meant losing my respectability."

"But you did it regardless."

"For God's sake, Ollie, I had no choice! I traded respectability for independence."

"Surely that wasn't the only reason."

"What else? Oh I see, you mean you think I'm an exhibitionist."

"You do like to be the center of attention."

"So I do. I did enjoy the life after I got used to it. But not at first. At first I was frightened. It's not an easy existence—going from town to town, never certain of the future. A young girl would have to be desperate to go into a career with so many dangers and hardships."

"You never told me that you became an actress out of desperation."

"Of course I did! My father left some money for us but it ran out within a year and we were destitute. A year after that my mother died and I was orphaned."

"You had no other family?"

"None who wanted anything to do with me. And anyway, I would have been too proud to throw myself on the mercy of strangers."

"Why did you never speak of this before, Marietta?"

"For the same reason that you never asked. Oh don't look so. Your thoughts were occupied elsewhere and so were mine. I didn't want your sympathy. I wanted you to think of me as beautiful and gay."

He sighed. "You were both those things, Marietta. I thought you were the loveliest creature I'd ever beheld."

"What about now, Ollie? Do you still think me beautiful."

"Yes."

She smiled and put her arms around his neck. "And you're still a handsome man of mystery. I was head over heels in love with you, Ollie. I didn't want to discuss my past. I only wanted to make love!"

"You had a strange way of showing it. You threw me over for another man."

"A rich man. I had no choice there, either. I left you because I needed some security."

"I would have taken care of you."

"Be realistic. You didn't have the money or the time. Sooner or later you would have left me. Admit it, Ollie, you wanted a fling with a pretty actress, not a lifetime commitment to a difficult woman with expensive tastes."

He was silent. Perhaps she was right. He had been crazy about her. But he hadn't had marriage on his mind.

She smiled knowingly. "I was a fool for you. I knew it could never work but I couldn't help myself."

"Hardly."

"Oh yes," she whispered. "You're as fascinating as you ever were. But you know that, don't you, Oliver? It's in the way you carry yourself. A woman likes a man with an edge to him, a dangerous man. Even if he's a danger to her."

"You're the dangerous one, Marietta."

"Am I?"

"You know you are."

Their gazes locked tight. She asked softly, "Do you like danger, Oliver?"

When he said nothing, she smiled again and drew his face to hers. "So do I," she whispered against his lips. "It's my weakness."

CHAPTER EIGHTEEN

A languorous morning breeze whispered over Oliver's flesh. He opened his eyes. A veil of cool flame draped his arm. Marietta's loosened hair.

His sleep-fogged brain dredged up last night's lovemaking and his gaze moved upward, taking in her closed lashes, the ivory curve of her cheek, the swell of her shoulders and naked breasts.

The bedroom door burst open. He snapped into a sitting position, then leaped from the bed.

Agatha Mussman pressed against the open doorframe. The preacher's skinny wife was trembling with strong emotion. Her gray skirts dragged wetly at her muddy boots. Her hair hung in damp strings around her corpse-pale face. She squeezed a Colt revolver between two outstretched hands. Her narrowed gaze traveled up and down Oliver's nude form. Her lips drew back from her clamped teeth.

"I should have known!" She shot a poisonous glance at Marietta who was now awake and sitting up in bed with the sheet drawn around her breasts. "Whore!"

Agatha pointed the gun at her. "You deserve to die just as you are, naked and rotten with the crawling maggots of disgusting lust!"

Oliver dived at her. He knocked the gun up just as it went off, drilling a bullet into the ceiling. The report rattled the hotel's walls. He forced Agatha to drop the weapon. Wrapping one arm tightly around her body, he flung the door closed with his free hand and dragged the coverlet off the bed.

Quelling Agatha was no easy matter. She bit his wrist. When he shook her loose she raked her sharp nails across his bare belly, drawing blood.

"You think to cover your shame with that blanket, but nothing will hide your sin from the eyes of God!" she shrieked. "You have been consorting with a harlot! May you both burn in the red hot flames of hell!"

Marietta was now out of bed and thrusting her arms through the sleeves of a silk wrapper. "Shut the woman up before she wakes the entire hotel!"

"Too late for that," Oliver muttered. His belly smarted from Agatha's attack. Holding her at arm's length, he struggled to cover himself. "Here, take her while I step into a pair of pants."

Agatha screeched, "Don't let the whore lay her filthy hands on me!"

Strangely, however, when Marietta seized Agatha's wrists the woman's frenzied resistance melted away. She sagged against the bed like a deflated balloon, then crumpled to the floor where she drew her knees up to her chest and lay moaning.

Oliver stepped into his pants and jerked on his shirt. He had just thrust its tails into his waistband when someone banged on the door.

A desk-clerk stood in the hall. He tried to see inside the room but Oliver, a full head taller and much wider in the chest and shoulders, blocked his view.

"Sorry to bother you sir, but one of our guests reports a commotion on this floor." When Oliver didn't respond, he added, "She claims to have heard screaming and what sounded like a gunshot."

"Indeed, as it happens I'm here because I heard the same thing and came to investigate," Oliver lied sternly. "Unfortunately, Miss Dumont had a slight accident. She had a nightmare, woke up screaming and fell out of bed. What may have sounded like a gunshot was actually her hand mirror hitting the nightstand. She apologizes for the disturbance."

The clerk stared in disbelief. The smell of exploding gunpowder still hung in the air. Agatha's faint moans and sniffles could be heard. Ignoring them, Oliver met the young man's skeptical gaze severely and won the staring match.

"So long as no one's been hurt."

"No one's been hurt. Miss Dumont is fine, just a bit rattled."

"I'll want to talk to her later. The hotel needs to guard its reputation for respectability."

"She'll be down to see you as soon as she's composed herself. Meanwhile, she's very sorry for the disturbance her bad dream caused. Put it down to the irregularity of her thespian lifestyle." When the clerk looked blank Oliver added, "Late hours and constant travel can result in troubled sleep."

The clerk walked to the staircase, glancing over his shoulder only once. Oliver remained at the door until he was out of sight and until the other cracked doors in the hallway finally closed.

He turned back to Marietta. She perched on the edge of the bed yanking on her stockings. "My irregular thespian lifestyle had nothing whatsoever to do with that." She pointed at the damaged ceiling.

Agatha lay on the floor, silent now except for soft weeping. Oliver knelt and looked down at her ravaged features. "What you just did was mad! You might have killed someone."

She sniveled.

"You don't want to do murder, do you? Surely that would be a worse sin than what you accuse me and Miss Dumont of."

Agatha squeezed her eyes shut and refused to answer.

"Why have you come like this?" he demanded. "Has something happened."

Agatha shuddered. "Leander," she whispered. "Leander is dead."

"When?"

"Early this morning. He just slipped away from me. He's left this sorry world and everything in it. Now I'm a widow."

Oliver felt Marietta's gaze on him and looked up. There was an odd expression on her face. Her lips turned down. "Not exactly," she said.

"What?"

"Agatha knows what I mean. That's why she's come here with a gun, the bloodthirsty bitch. She wanted to kill me because I know the truth about her."

"What are you talking about?"

"Holier than thou Agatha is not Leander Mussman's widow nor ever could be. When he shacked up with Agatha he already had a wife."

Agatha let out a shriek of renewed rage and scrambled into a sitting position. "Evil, evil woman!"

"Evil am I? I'm not the one whose been living with a married man. It's you, Agatha, who is the biggest sinner in this room. You must have known all along that Leander was a bigamist."

"I knew no such thing. And it's not true! It can't be! Leander was a saint! You're not fit to lick his shoes."

Marietta threw her head back and laughed long and loud. "You can't have known your pretend-husband very well. Leander thought me and every other pretty woman he met fit to lick a good many things. He was a philanderer on and off the stage. Preaching didn't change him. Not one bit!"

"Liar!" Agatha struggled to get at Marietta.

Oliver restrained her. "What's this all about?"

"That whore came here to blackmail my husband!"

Marietta said, "No such thing! Running into Leander on this island was pure coincidence." Turning her back to them, she searched through the wardrobe, finally extracting a light blue dress with a striped skirt.

Oliver looked from one maddening woman to the other. "Will someone please explain what's going on?"

Marietta shook out the skirt and then dropped it over her head. "It's simple enough. The last time I saw Leander he was married to Carmen Reed."

"Carmen Reed?"

"An actress with a figure that seemed to drive men wild. It certainly had that effect on Leander. She's told me how he did everything he could think of to seduce her. When she wouldn't give in he finally married her and that did the trick."

"Liar!" Agatha screeched.

Marietta shrugged into a jacket. "The ceremony was performed by a small town Justice of the Peace. It wasn't much, but as far as I know it was legal."

"Are you sure of this?" Oliver asked.

"Of course I'm sure. Carmen and Leander parted years ago, but they never divorced. She nearly fell over when she saw him."

"Saw him when?"

"Three days ago."

"You mean she's here on the island?"

"Carmen's playing the part of Helena in Midsummer Night's Dream. You can imagine her reaction when she spotted Leander and found out he'd become a preacher of all things." Marietta snorted. "She asked me to talk to him for her."

"About what?"

"About helping her out. Carmen's down on her luck and he owes her."

"She wanted you to blackmail him for her?"

Marietta stamped her foot. "Not at all. She had no interest in ruining his setup. When they were together he was always out of money. That's one of the reasons why she left him. He would sneak out of town in the middle of the night and stick her with the hotel bills. She was thrilled to find he'd become prosperous and hoped he'd pay a few of her debts. They are legally married, after all."

Agatha glared. "It's a lie! Leander's only other wife was Hermione's mother and she died when Hermione was a baby."

"Leander is legally married to Carmen, and she's very much alive. If Leander left any sort of estate, it's Carmen who'll get it!"

Agatha's scream shook the hotel's walls. She collapsed on the floor writhing like an eel in shock.

CHAPTER NINETEEN

After disguising the bullet hole in Marietta's ceiling with white greasepaint, Oliver escorted Agatha to Gibralter. He left her with Hermione and went up to the big house where Jay Cooke ushered him into his library. It was a handsome room with elaborately carved woodwork and a stunning view of the lake.

"What a sad time this is for that poor family," Cooke said, shaking his gray head so that his long, fluffy beard seemed to tremble in sympathy. "I didn't know Leander Mussman well, but as a Christian I feel duty-bound to shepherd his widow and orphaned daughter through this melancholic period."

"I imagine Agatha Mussman will want to return Leander's body to his Temple of Redemption in Toledo."

"That will be done, of course. My caretaker, Owen Brown, is making arrangements. However, Agatha has requested a memorial service be held on Gull Island."

Oliver felt his brows jump up. "The island Mussman was hoping to purchase?"

"Exactly. Despite every discouragement he was intent on establishing his community on that barren spot. Now, of course, such notions must be set aside. Agatha seems to think the island will make an appropriate location for a ceremony of final leave-taking."

"Do you mean taking leave of Leander or of his scheme to establish a religious community?"

"Both, I suppose." Cooke shrugged. "I'm not sure Gull island can accommodate her wishes. It won't be easy to assemble Mrs. Mussman's guests on such a wild and inaccessible dot of land."

"You've visited the place?"

"Never. I've fished off all of the Lake Erie islands and explored most of them but I've never ventured onto Gull."

"Why not? It's less than a day's sail from here."

"True, but then so are many more tempting places to visit. I've only heard Gull described as the home of snakes and a multitude of noxious insects. Before I support Mrs. Mussman's wish to go there with a party of mourners I must get in touch with the owners."

"Who are the owners?"

Cooke steepled his fingers. "To the best of my knowledge Gull Island was purchased some fifty years ago by a consortium of vintners. They had planned to grow grapes for winemaking but after a brief period abandoned the place as unsuitable for agriculture. There's almost no fresh water to be had and the wild birds drop so much lime that they kill off the vegetation. Gull Island has been derelict for half a century."

Oliver stared out the window. Beyond the tall trees shading the yard the lake sparkled like a sapphire in sunlight. "Sounds as if it wouldn't have made good ground for a religious community."

"That was my opinion but Leander, poor soul, was a dreamer. He believed he could create paradise where nothing else would grow. If the owners are agreeable to using Gull for his Memorial Service I'll visit the property to make a determination as to its suitability. If you get the chance, perhaps you'll do the same."

"I will."

"Good. Then we'll both have done our best for our poor departed friend."

Soon after this discussion Oliver returned to Put-In-Bay to keep his caving appointment. On his way to Brown's home he ran into Billy Stojack leading a skinny pony by a length of frayed rope.

"Is that Professor Paradise's diving horse you've got?"

"Sure is." Billy grinned and then returned his attention to the faltering pony. The animal appeared to be in sad shape, trembling and so weak that it was barely able to put one hoof in front of the other.

"He looks terrible. What's wrong with him?"

"You'd look terrible if you'd had nothing to eat or drink for nigh on two days."

"The horse has been starved?"

"Professor Paradise hasn't been around to tend him and nobody else neither. He'd have died if I hadn't come."

"What happened to the professor?"

"Don't know. Mrs. Farris, the lady who runs the taffy shop, thinks he took off 'cause he wasn't making much money here. She's the one told me about the pony."

Billy had coaxed the stumbling animal around a heap of spilled stone.

"Where are you taking it?"

"To home. We got a shed in back. I can keep him there. Always did want to have my own horse."

"Will that be all right with your mother? It costs money to care for a horse, even a small one like this."

Billy shot Oliver a rueful look. "Maybe I won't tell Ma right off. Not until I figure out how I'm going to buy feed."

Oliver gave the horse's bony rump a pat and then withdrew several bills from his pocket. "This will help get you started."

"Golly, you mean it?"

"I mean it."

Billy crammed the bills into his overalls and flashed Oliver a dazzling smile. "Gee, thanks! This'll go a long way to feeding Blossom. I guess you must like horses."

"I was your age once. I dreamed of having my own horse but never had the money for it."

Billy squinted at Oliver, obviously struggling to imagine him as ever having been a young boy. He asked, "You have your own horse now?"

"No."

"How come? Still can't afford one?"

In fact, with Chloe's expenses and William Pinkerton's loan to repay Oliver couldn't afford to keep a horse. He said, "I live in a city where it's easier to rent an animal if you need one. I hope you can keep Blossom. The poor beast has had a hard life. Professor Paradise should be horsewhipped for leaving a dumb animal to starve."

"It's strange he would act so mean," Billy agreed. "Seemed like a nice enough fella'. I'd never have thought he'd be so cruel." He shrugged. "Once I get Blossom home and feed him up he'll be fine. Where you going?"

Oliver explained his appointment to go caving with Brown and Venator.

Billy said, "Them two been wriggling through all the caves on the island like regular old water snakes searching out a nest. They're just about done by now. Fact is, I hear Mr. Venator is going back to Germany tomorrow."

"You hear a lot, don't you Billy?"

"Ain't much that goes on gets past me," Billy agreed with a boastful laugh. "If you don't get to see enough caves this afternoon just call on me. I know all the caves on this island. I can show you whatever you want to see."

"I'll keep that in mind."

They parted and a few minutes later Oliver turned into a long lane enclosed on both sides by lush rows of grapevines. He took off his jacket and slung it over his shoulder. A moment later he stopped to roll up his shirtsleeves. The sun warming his forearms sparkled on the ripening fruit. A musky scent pervaded the warm summer air. Bees hummed in the shadows of thick green leaves. A garter snake slithered into a tuft of tall grass.

The lane led to a solid looking house situated on a large piece of property. Oliver paused to admire its fine stretch of lakefront screened by cottonwoods.

John Brown Junior had been involved in almost as many abolitionist projects as his notorious father. Yet he had survived his family's tragic ordeal and become a prosperous man. Rumors alleged that after the senior Brown's execution for treason his abolitionist backers had financed the eldest son. Whether that was true or not it was clear that Brown Junior had done well for himself.

He and Venator were waiting for Oliver on the porch. Both men wore old cotton shirts and rough trousers held up by suspenders.

"So, you're game to go exploring with us," Brown said. He levered himself up from a weathered rocking chair. "How do you feel about squeezing through tight spots?"

"I've been in a few of them before and managed," Oliver said with a slight smile.

Brown laughed. "As have we all. But cavers, they're a special breed. Don't you agree, Emil?"

Venator nodded. "Oh yes, it takes a bit of madness to go crawling through the caves."

Oliver thought of a cave that had saved his life. It had happened in West Virginia during his days as a Union sharpshooter. He'd stumbled on the grotto while trying to elude a unit of Rebel soldiers hunting him. The shallow cavern had been little more than a dank hole in the mountain, but it had been a godsend. He'd disguised its entrance with bushes and crouched behind them with his rifle loaded and ready. The Confederates had passed within inches and hadn't discovered him.

"There are some truly stunning caves on our Mother Earth," Venator went on. "I've seen places filled with crystals and spectacular formations. But most are just holes in the ground. It takes a bit of a madman to see the fascination in those. And then, of course, there's the danger."

"Danger?"

Venator winked. "There's always the element of peril in caving. Especially this is true in unexplored caves. Anything can happen in such places. One should never go into a cave alone. And, of course, it's most vital to have the correct equipment."

"Are the caves on this island dangerous?"

Brown laughed and slapped Venator on the back. "Emil here is just funning you. We've already explored most of the caves that interest us. They're dark and musty, perhaps, but not risky. We wouldn't take you where there was danger. Today we plan to revisit an exposed vein of strontium in a cave on the Herbster property. Does that interest you?"

"Very much. Although, I am curious to see the cave where you found signs that somebody had been camping recently."

"That's on the Herbster property, but you won't find it of much interest."

"Nevertheless, I'd like to see it."

"Then come along. I've put all the equipment you'll need into the wagon, so we're ready to go."

A few minutes later they were rolling past the grape vines with the afternoon sun hot on their heads. As Brown turned the wagon onto the road he began a lecture on the geology of Lake Erie.

"The islands are what remain of a ridge created by slow-moving glaciers."

"When the ice melted it created Lake Erie?"

"Yes, but before that happened ice rivers cut deeply around the hard rock of the islands, leaving them in relief above the present lake level."

"How were the caves formed?"

"Most likely water seeping into the rock dissolved away layers of calcium and other soluble materials."

Oliver remembered Waterman's description of the island as a honeycomb. He asked, "Are the caves interconnected?"

"At some level I suppose they must be. Only the fish can say for sure as most connections are below water."

Oliver pictured a honeycomb, its dark web of passages reaching far below the island's surface. What would it be like to be trapped in such a dank prison?

He said, "Indians inhabited this territory long before the white man. The caves must have been known to them."

"Oh, indeed." Brown tapped the horse's reins. "Human skeletons have been found in the caves. In once instance it appeared that the unfortunate individual got a foot caught in the rocks and was unable to escape."

"These were Indian skeletal remains?"

"It's likely."

"Likely but not certain?" Venator queried.

"Who can tell how old a skeleton might be? It's possible that some adventurous white settler got trapped."

Venator said, "Men have been known to disappear mysteriously, have they not? In town they still talk of those tourists from Virginia who vanished and were never found."

Brown nodded. "They were brothers named Woodley. It's presumed they were drowned."

Venator said, "But perhaps they were murdered, or trapped in a cave like the Indian and unable to escape."

Brown looked disgruntled. "Highly unlikely."

"But not impossible." Venator giggled. "The Woodleys were southerners, were they not?"

"Confederates who'd served time in Johnson's Island and were planning some kind of ex-prisoner Encampment here on Put-In-Bay."

"What a fine whodunit. The brothers Woodley come here to make arrangements for an Encampment and, pouf, they vanish from the face of the earth. Perhaps we'll solve the mystery of it this afternoon."

"How is that?" Brown asked.

"Perhaps we'll find their remains in the cave we explore. Won't that be exciting?"

CHAPTER TWENTY

Despite Venator's forecast, the afternoon's caving proved disappointing for Oliver. He'd been intrigued by the idea that Frank Aballo might be using a cave for a hiding place. But whoever had left the old blanket and empty tins of food in the Herbster cave had clearly abandoned the location. The Herbster cave was visited too frequently its owner and Brown and Venator to be a satisfactory hiding place for a fugitive.

The vein of Strontium running through the location fascinated Oliver's companions. Venator was certain the strontium could be profitably mined. Not long after he and Brown arrived at the property they sat down with the owner to discuss a lease for mining rights.

Left to kick his heels, Oliver wandered across the road to a neighboring cave. Brown had described this sister cave opposite the Herbster property as being large, studded with stalagmites, and containing a subterranean channel filled with lake water. He'd explained that it was called "Perry's Cave" because islanders believed Admiral Perry had explored it during the War of 1812. A wooden building that had been built over its entrance advertised tours for ten cents.

Oliver arrived at the entrance in time to join a party of school children just beginning a tour. An hour later he rejoined his companions. They had concluded their business and were in an expansive mood.

"What did you think of Perry's Cave?" Brown inquired.

"Impressive. I can see why Perry might have chosen it for a hiding spot." With its high ceilings and copious supply of fresh drinking water Perry's cave would also make an excellent hidey-hole for a bank robber. Oliver wondered if there were other such caves on the island, caves unknown to tourists. If so, Aballo might have spent a night in the Herbster cave and then gone in search of one more private.

Unfortunately, Venator and Brown, deeply involved in concluding their business dealings, would clearly be no help.

They offered to convey Oliver back into town and buy him a drink. He declined and set off on foot in the opposite direction. He had judged himself to be within a half hour walk to Waterman's cabin. Forty-five minutes later, trudging along an overgrown lane and swatting biting flies, he acknowledged to himself that he'd lost his way.

He mopped his perspiring forehead. It was late afternoon and hot. The sun burned fiercely through the leaves and cast sharp black shadows. A sluggish breeze moved through the treetops. Otherwise only the metallic buzz of cicadas disturbed the green and gold silence.

Oliver's ears picked up a faint tuneless whistling. A moment later the whistling was accompanied by the crunch and rustle of careless footfalls. Billy Stojack sauntered around a bend. When he saw Oliver he waved and trotted up.

"Mr. Redcastle! What you doing here?"

"Getting lost. What about you?"

"Oh, I ain't lost." Billy chuckled at the notion. "I'm going swimming."

"Swimming? Here in the woods? Why aren't you swimming in town?"

"I don't like that beach. Too dirty and too many people. I got my own private spot. Want me to show you?"

"I'd be honored."

Oliver brushed away a mosquito. Hot and sweaty as he felt, a swim sounded like a grand idea. He fell into step with Billy who led him down a winding path ever deeper into the woods.

Oliver asked, "How's Blossom doing?"

"Okay I think. I watered him good and fed him some oats I bought with that money you gave me. I ain't told Ma yet."

"You'll have to tell her soon. She's bound to notice there's a horse in her shed."

Billy shook his head. "You know, I just can't understand why Professor Paradise would act like he did. I asked around the docks and nobody remembers seeing him leave."

"Could he be lost or injured somewhere?"

"Injured, maybe. You'd have to be touched in the head to get lost on the island. This time of day all you got to do is head where the sun's going down and that'll take you back to town. You probably had that figured."

"Actually," Oliver said, "I was looking for Gene Waterman's place. I know its somewhere around these parts."

"We go right past." A few minutes later Billy stopped where a narrow horse trail diverged from the main trail. "Waterman's cabin is in there."

Oliver took a step or two but Billy didn't move. He said, "I can't go in with you. Last year he caught me on his beach and near skinned me alive."

"Sounds as if you're not partial to him."

"Nobody likes Mr. Waterman. He's sneaky and he bad- mouths people. You can visit him if you want, but not me."

"That's all right. I'll look him up later. Let's go to your swimming hole."

They continued on for another ten minutes until their path opened onto a rocky plateau with a spectacular view of the lake below. "That's where I swim," Billy said, pointing to a pebbled beach at the foot of the cliff. I know the man who owns it and he don't care."

Together they climbed down, slipping and sliding over loose rock, using tufts of weeds for handholds. Oliver could see why Billy preferred this inviting beach to the one in town. Wildflowers grew out of the stone walls enclosing it and water clear as glass lapped over a carpet of multi-colored pebbles.

The pebbles were hard on Oliver's bare feet, but once he and Billy were afloat that mild discomfort was forgotten.

"Nice, ain't it," Billy said as he splashed about.

"Wonderful!" Oliver put his head back and let the water cradle him. As his cotton union suit floated around him like a ghostly second skin he squinted up into the sky. Only one small puff of white cloud marred its burning blue perfection. The limestone cliffs ringing the beach were capped with a matt of greenery that seemed to glow in the late afternoon light. An egret took off from a ledge, its wings spread wide, its long neck and legs stretched like a ballet dancer's.

Oliver began a lazy backstroke around the edge of the stone outcroppings. Noticing a place where the stone was worn away in an arch he paddled closer to investigate. The arch had been cut deep into the rock, narrowing into a dark gap. He put his feet down in the chest high water and pointed.

"What's that?"

Billy dog-paddled to his side. "There's a cave in there but you got to swim in underwater to get to it. I got a friend whose brother did it. But he's a real strong swimmer and can hold his breath more than two minutes. I tried once and near drowned."

"Really. What did he say about the cave?"

"Not much. He didn't stay. He only went in on a dare. When his mama found out she promised to lick him if he ever did it again."

Oliver cocked his head. He was not a strong swimmer himself. Nevertheless, on impulse, he dived underwater and began paddling into the dark, narrow entrance.

The water was clear enough so that he could make out where he was going. But once he was inside the hole all light disappeared. Blinded, he started to back out. A surge slammed him against the rough stone. His head hit the roof of the narrow passage. He gasped, filling his lungs with water in the process.

CHAPTER TWENTY-ONE

"Mr Redcastle! Oh please wake up!" Billy Stojack sat on Oliver's back, pumping at his chest and shoulders like a fireman bent on saving a burning building.

Billy's weight pressed Oliver into a bed of wet pebbles. The skin on his ribs was scraped raw. He felt as if he'd been dumped head over heels into a washtub and beaten by a violent laundress.

"Are you okay Mr. Redcastle?"

Oliver groaned.

"You're alive!" Billy crowed.

"What happened?"

"Don't know. Guess you got stuck."

"Stuck underwater?"

"Yep. When you didn't come up I dived after you. It's lucky you were wearing that white Union suit. I grabbed onto it and pulled you out."

Oliver groaned. Inches from his nose a dead fish was beached on a mound of stinking weed. It dawned on him that if it weren't for this boy he'd be in the same condition.

"I'm a damn fool!"

"Alls well that ends well," Billy allowed cheerfully.

"Where'd you hear that?"

"Ma took me to a Shakespeare play. I shoulda' mentioned that the boy who swam into that underwater cave was kind of a runt. A big man like you trying the same thing was sure to get stuck."

Billy rolled off and Oliver struggled to his hands and knees. After coughing up a stream of rank lake water he fell over on his back and put a clammy arm over his eyes. He felt nauseous.

"How you feeling now?" Billy inquired anxiously.

"Fine."

"You don't look fine. Look kinda' green."

"I'll be all right. Just need a few minutes."

"You think you'll be okay to walk back into town by yourself?"

"Yes."

"'Cause I got to go pretty soon." Billy shot an anxious look over his shoulder. "Shoulda' been back half hour ago. Ma doesn't know I took off pulling weeds to go for a swim. She finds out she'll be so mad she won't let me keep Blossom."

"Then you'd better get back to those weeds."

"You sure? I wouldn't want you to die or nothin'."

"I'll be fine, Billy. You get back home."

After Billy scrambled up the cliff Oliver lay still, letting the sun dry out his wet underwear and warm his skin. Gradually he felt less like death. He squinted at the sky. It was still a fine cerulean blue, but the trees above cast long shadows on the stone beach.

He sat up, tested his arms and legs and then got to his feet. The climb up from the water's edge took considerably more effort than the slide down had. He found his discarded clothing, dressed quickly and then stood for several moments orienting himself. When he felt sure of his direction he retraced his steps and turned into the path that Billy had claimed would lead him to Waterman's place. Originally he had planned to ask Waterman for more information about the island's caves. Now he just wanted a ride back to town.

After following the narrow, overgrown track for ten minutes he wondered if he'd mis-remembered the direction. The track finally widened and he spotted the familiar tumbledown cabin at the far end of the clearing.

There was no sign of Waterman's horse and wagon. The only sound was the slosh of waves below the cliff and the drone of cicadas. The shadows had lengthened alarmingly. Squinting at the lowering sun Oliver realized he had barely an hour of light left. It would take him at least that long to walk into town. Not a pleasant prospect considering how tender he felt in every bone and muscle.

Sighing, he started to turn away when a movement in the brush caught his eye. He looked hard into the murky undergrowth. A cat slunk out of a patch of Queen Anne's lace. Oliver recognized the scruffy tabby he'd seen on Waterman's property the night he'd arrived.

Once in the open it accelerated into a blur of black and gray fur. Then it was gone. The cat had vanished as if by magic. Oliver approached the spot where it had disappeared and perceived a thicket of weeds disguising a hole in the ground. Once he dislodged the weeds he saw that the opening looked large enough that a man might try lowering himself into it.

Given his near-death experience earlier he was disinclined to do this but curious enough to investigate further. He was about to kneel and peer into the hole when he heard the crunch of wagon wheels. He kicked the weeds back into place and walked toward the noise.

A horse and wagon emerged from the trees. Gene Waterman sat atop the wagon holding the reins with a slack hand. His jaw dropped when he saw Oliver.

"What you doing poking around my property?"

"Looking for you."

"Well, I wasn't here."

"Now you are, and I'm glad of it. I had a mishap while swimming and would appreciate a ride into town."

Waterman guffawed. "You're all over bruises and scrapes. Looks to me as if you been pokin' your nose into spots where it wasn't welcome."

Oliver rubbed the back of his neck. "You're right about the bruises. I don't feel much like hoofing it back to my hotel."

"I'll give you a lift, though it ain't what I had planned for my evening. Climb aboard."

With some difficulty, Oliver hoisted himself onto the wagon. When it was rolling toward Catawba Avenue Waterman shot Oliver a sly sideways glance and said, "I just come from town. Picked up some news that might interest you."

"What's that?"

"Maybe you already heard it but the preacher Mussman kicked the bucket."

"It was all over the island this morning."

"Well, chew on this. Widow Mussman's mighty upset. Turns out the bible thumper was a bigamist, married to more than one woman."

"Agatha has good reason to be upset. Leander's daughter is to inherit Gabriel Goggins' fortune. Agatha expected to control the money until Hermione's twenty-first birthday."

"Not if she wasn't married legal." Waterman hooted. "That's one lucky girl, getting money from Goggins. Likely her pa died broker than my piggy bank."

"You have a piggy bank?"

Waterman poked Oliver's sore shoulder. "What did you think I was putting my big Pinkerton wages into?"

"No idea. I'm still waiting for you to earn them."

"I'm earning my pay this very minute. Ain't I carting you back into town when I'd rather be snug at home with a good book and a bottle of comfort."

"You read books?"

"Of course!" He scowled. "Look here, Redcastle, I ain't the no-account trash to take me for. I come from an educated family. If it weren't for the hard times I run into I would have had a good future ahead of me."

"Stop feeling sorry for yourself. The future's always ahead of a man."

"Who do you think you are, telling me what I should feel?"

Oliver shrugged. "You're right. Forget I said it. What you choose to do with your life is none of my business."

"That's the truth and don't you forget it!"

Both men were silent for several minutes. The cart wheels ground irritably on the road bed as the shadows thickened around them.

Waterman cleared his throat and said, "Anyhow, that ain't what I want to talk about. Matter of fact, it's lucky we met like this. I was looking for you in town."

"You were?"

"Soon as possible we should get out to Gull Island."

"Why?"

"Aballo may have buried his train-robbing loot there."

"What makes you say so?"

"Something I heard while I was poking around in the harbor." Waterman flicked the reins. "Something I seen with my own eyes."

"What are you talking about?"

"Young fella meeting Aballo's description hired a boat and sailed off for Gull a couple days back with a big black suitcase. He's since left the island. Least he ain't around anymore. When he arrived he was carrying that big black suitcase."

"How do you know?"

"I seen it myself."

"Why didn't you mention this before?"

"Didn't think anything of it until now. Anyhow, down at the waterfront they're saying he left Put-In Bay empty-handed. Now I call that mighty odd."

"You think the suitcase contained the money we're looking for and that he buried it on Gull?"

"Could be."

"Why would he bury it there?"

"Why wouldn't he? Place is deserted. Nobody goes to Gull. He can't carry the loot around with him, can he? If I was you I'd get out to that island with a shovel double quick. We're not the only ones curious about what was in that suitcase."

"Who else is curious?"

"Look here, the islanders ain't stupid. They know you're not an ordinary tourist. They know you're looking for something or somebody. That train robbery has been in all the papers. Don't take a genius to put two and two together. If I was you I'd get over to Gull when nobody's looking."

"When would that be?"

Waterman glanced up at the purpling sky. "Late tonight, maybe. After everyone's asleep. Here's my idea."

CHAPTER TWENTY-TWO

Six hours later Oliver said, "Half the night in this rotten tub and we've barely cleared Gibralter."

Waterman adjusted Pretty Girl's sail. "That's the trouble with you city slickers. No patience."

"I've shown the patience of a saint. Sneaking out of my hotel in the dead of night! A man should be in his bed at this ungodly hour."

Waterman snickered. "Or in someone else's bed. It's all over town you was visiting that redheaded actress last night, and there was a ruckus with Mussman's widow."

Ignoring that, Oliver asked, "Do you think we'll reach Gull Island by dawn?"

"Should get there easy. Wind is picking up."

Oliver tried to find a comfortable spot next to the tiller. His bruises pained him more than they had earlier that evening when Waterman had talked him into this escapade.

"I hope you're right about our man. If we find he's hidden the loot on Gull our work is done."

"Pinkerton's don't care about catching Aballo?"

"It's the money we're hired to recoup."

"So if we find it you go home to Baltimore and we've seen the last of each other."

"That's it."

"Sounds mighty good to me."

"Me too, if you're right."

Waterman spat and wiped his nose on his sleeve. "I know I'm right. Ain't no other explanation for why a man would take a valise to that godforsaken island. Anyhow, we have to take a look-see."

"I suppose so."

"And we had to do it in the dark so nobody would be the wiser."

"I suppose that makes sense."

Oliver suspected this moonlit trip across the lake was a wild goose chase. What's more, he didn't like Waterman's attitude. From the first enlisting the man's cooperation had been like dragging a recalcitrant mule up the vertical side of a cliff. Yet he'd been eager to sail to Gull in the dead of night. Why so enthusiastic? Oliver moved his legs restlessly. The back of his neck prickled.

"About that redheaded actress. . ."

"I'm not interested in discussing Miss Dumont."

"Miss Dumont, is it? I bet that ain't what you called her when you was visiting her room t'other night. Wouldn't mind visiting her room myself. Don't suppose she'd welcome the likes of me, though. Women with her looks can be mighty hoity-toity."

"There appear to be plenty of females on this island. Surely by now you've found yourself one."

Waterman cast Oliver an unfriendly look. "Mind yer own business."

"You mind yours then."

They sailed for another half hour in hostile silence. The creak of the tiller and gurgle of moving water beneath the keel put Oliver in a dreamlike state. He began to think about Marietta and last night's lovemaking.

Whatever else there might be between them there had always been heat. Her inexcusable behavior and the long years since they'd been young lovers hadn't quenched that. It was like a subterranean peat fire, smoldering in the dark but ready to flare at the least breath of oxygen.

In the course of his peripatetic life—as a soldier, then as a Pinkerton detective, then as a private investigator--Oliver had cared for other women. But, he admitted to himself, he'd never been in love with anyone in quite the same besotted fashion that he'd adored Marietta.

What about the devilish woman turned him into such a fool, he wondered. It wasn't just her beauty. Even while condemning her unscrupulous amorality, he admired Marietta's independence, her strength of spirit, her ability to do whatever it took to survive.

He compared her to his mother. She'd been a strong, intelligent woman. Yet she'd tied herself to a husband who'd led her into misery and poverty. Marietta would never settle for life in a barren cabin with a man so obsessed by heaven that he never saw the dirt under his feet.

Oliver considered his daughter. What kind of woman would Chloe become? What kind of woman did he want her to become? Would he desire her to be self-sacrificing in the way that had eventually worn his mother out and killed her? Or would he prefer that she have some of Marietta's strength and independence?

"There 'tis," Waterman said.

Oliver roused himself to peer under the sail. Rays of faint gray light picked out a dark hump that rose above the waterline like the wrinkled shell of a mollusc. "Gull Island?"

"The same."

"Not very big."

"No more than ten acres. How that preacher thought he could set up Paradise on such a godforsaken lump of rock is beyond me. Man was a fool. Daughter now, she's something else."

"What do you mean?"

"Hermione Mussman is one smart little girl. Gets herself engaged to a rich man, then buries him and inherits his loot. That's what I call intelligent."

"Intelligence has nothing to do with it. The chit was nowhere near Goggins when he drowned."

"Her bankrobber lover might have been."

"You think Hermione and Aballo arranged to drown Goggins?"

Waterman shrugged. "It's an idea."

"I think somebody cut into Goggins' mast. I know somebody rammed his vessel in the storm. I don't know if it was the same person, though. It couldn't have been Hermione. She doesn't know one end of a boat from the other. Until today I had no reason to think Aballo knew boats, either. But you tell me he rented a sailboat and got here on his own to bury the loot. So maybe he did engineer the accident that drowned Goggins."

Waterman shrugged. "We got to tack one more time if we're going to make the island. Watch your head."

The sail swung and Pretty Girl changed course. The sun was above the horizon when Waterman dropped the anchor and the two men waded ashore. In the early dawn light Oliver saw a narrow stone beach littered with deadwood. A tangle of low-growing greenery straggled along its edges. A few decent size trees bristled on the island's interior, but most of what grew on it was scrub.

"Not exactly a Garden of Eden."

Waterman snorted. "Pile of barren stone. Only thing can live here is snakes and spiders."

"I see no sign that Aballo visited."

"You expect he left a calling card? We ain't had much of a look. Let's take a walk along the beach."

Waterman set off toward a dolomite outcropping. Oliver followed. When they climbed to the top Waterman pointed. "See that?"

Rocks had been piled up into a little hill. Oliver squinted at them.

"Looks like someone made some kind of marker. Maybe your train robber left a calling card after all."

"Why would he?"

"Why ask me? I ain't got no crystal ball. Let's go have a closer look."

They stumbled along the serrated shoreline, skirting the carcasses of rotting fish. Oliver's feet crunched over bleached bird skeletons. Wolf spiders skittered across the white stones and disappeared into crevasses.

A tangle of snakes lay sunning on a flat rock. Waterman paused to throw a stone and mutter curses.

"Why bother?" Oliver asked. "They're not poisonous."

"They'll bite a man."

"Only if provoked."

Waterman shuddered. "Hate snakes! Can't abide the damned things! Had one crawl into my bed one night while I was still building my cabin and didn't have a door on the place. Still gives me nightmares."

Oliver stared at his cohort, thinking he was an odd blend. He tried to appear rough and tough, yet he was sensitive as a girl about some things.

Waterman said, "I bet Aballo's train loot is buried under them rocks."

"Not unless he's a fool. He wouldn't put treasure anywhere so obvious."

"People don't always think straight. Maybe he wanted to make sure he could find it."

They approached to within a few feet of the odd construction. Waterman said, "Got to be a reason why these rocks are piled up."

"Yes."

"One of us has to investigate."

"Go ahead."

"That's right, make me do all the work." He kicked at the rocks. Half a dozen tumbled over and he peered into the hole he'd made. "Whooeee! Lookee here!"

"What do you see?"

"See for yourself. I ain't going to do it all for you!"

Cautiously, Oliver stepped forward. Something metallic glinted inside the hole. He dropped onto one knee to fish it out when instinct warned him. Half-squatting, he turned his head and saw Waterman bearing down on him with a driftwood club. He was able to shift his weight in time to avoid the full force of the blow that knocked him sprawling across the shale.

He grunted a protest and rolled as Waterman struck again, clipping him on the shoulder.

"Ha! Got you that time. Now I'll get you good!" Swinging the club like a bat, Waterman came after him. Oliver scrambled into a crouch. He seized a stone and threw it with all his strength. The missile hit Waterman squarely between the eyes and he staggered backward.

Oliver got to his feet. He was about to lunge at his attacker when he saw the gun. Waterman had reached into his shirt and pulled out a derringer apparently holstered under his armpit.

Oliver had no weapon. Pivoting, he raced toward the nearest tree. He'd made no more than a dozen steps when he felt the hot sting of fire in his thigh and knew he'd been hit. He kept moving, swerving from side to side in case Waterman was carrying a two shot weapon.

Waterman fired again but this time the bullet went wide, kicking up dust a full yard from Oliver's flying feet. He reached the tree and pressed up against the side hidden from his attacker's view. It wouldn't take long for Waterman to reload.

"You can't hide from me, Redcastle. I know you got a bullet in you. How's it feel to be on the wrong end of a gun barrel? Say your prayers. I'm coming after you!"

Oliver heard the crunch of Waterman's approaching feet. He looked around for some means to defend himself. Near his right ankle he saw a crooked stick, black in color similar in appearance to the serpents slithering through the rocks. He picked it up.

"I've got a snake here. Come close enough and you'll get it in your face."

The feet stilled. "You're lying."

"Try me." Oliver waved the upper part of the stick, trying to make it look alive. He crumbled a handful of dead leaves to mimic the sound of rattles. It seemed like a hopeless charade but Waterman surprised him by giving a hollow laugh and backing off.

"Why should I waste another bullet on you? Nobody ever visits Gull. Now that Mussman's gone nobody ever will. All alone here you'll either bleed to death or starve. Good riddance."

Oliver listened to Waterman's retreating feet. He peered around the tree trunk and watched him climb into the boat and sail away. He slumped onto the ground and looked at his blood-soaked leg.

CHAPTER TWENTY-THREE

The blazing sun promised a smoldering day and Oliver's throat was already dry as hot grit. Glumly, he watched Pretty Girl's sail disappear over the horizon and his canteen of water with it.

He sank onto his haunches, wedged his back against the trunk of a half dead tree and used his penknife to cut away the bloodied section of his pant leg. After examining the wound he tore the sleeve from his shirt and began shredding it for bandages.

Biting flies buzzed around his injury. He batted a half dozen away and cursed Waterman. What a fool he'd been to turn his back on the man! But why had the villain lured him to this godforsaken spot and then attacked? What did he have to gain?

Oliver sat still for several minutes, steeling himself for what he had to do next. Waterman's Derringer had been little more than a pea-shooter. The bullet hadn't shattered the bone or even gone very far into the flesh. Gingerly Oliver touched the lesion and felt the shape of the slug beneath the pad of his finger. It would have to come out.

In the course of a recent investigation he had spent time in the company of a doctor who believed in a new theory of antisepsis. According to this newfangled notion tiny invisible creatures existed in the air that could invade an open wound and eventually produce gangrene. During the war Oliver had watched men die of gangrene. Starvation would be preferable.

He fished a box of matches out of his pocket. Fortunately he carried them, unfortunately there were only three left. He lit one and held the knife blade in the flame until it burned his fingers. Then he cut out the bullet. He batted away more flies and tied two of the strips from his sleeve around the injury. After that he lay back and fainted.

Thirst and the throbbing of his leg dragged him from unconsciousness. The sun had found his face and burned it raw. The flies were making a meal of him. He'd be eaten alive if he continued lying on the ground like deadwood.

Despite his sore leg he managed to get to his feet and hobble to the water's edge. He bathed his sunburned face and neck and stood staring longingly down at the wavelets lapping around his shoes. He could drink from the lake, of course, but figured he'd soon be belly sick if he did. On the other hand, he needed water and he needed it soon. That was worth the sacrifice of another match.

He gathered sticks to make a fire. Earlier he'd noticed a rusty tin can washed up on the beach. He cleaned that out as best he could, dipped it into the lake and set it in the hot coals. He steeped some wild mint in the boiling water. After it cooled, he used part of it to wash and re-bandage his wound and then drank the remainder slowly.

The liquid helped him clear his mind. He endeavored to consider his situation dispassionately. People said this island had no fresh water but perhaps they were wrong. Perhaps if he explored he'd find a spring or even a cave that would provide shelter. Whatever the case, he told himself he had to do something. He set off toward the interior of the island.

His goal was a high spot crowned by a tuft of scrubby trees. He figured that once he got there he'd get a better idea of the island's terrain. A hundred yards inland, however, he regretted the decision.

The day was true to its earlier vow of turning into a scorcher. Gull island, with only a few scanty trees for cover, was an anvil for the sun's blistering hammer.

Flies, mosquitoes and a myriad of other insects buzzed and crawled in the rocks and patches of weed. They seemed to thrive on the oppressive heat and tormented Oliver's every limping step. He swatted at them, lost his balance and disturbed a nest of snakes. The angry hum of their rattles sent him scrambling.

When he had limped a safe distance away from the hissing, writhing snakes he stopped to mop his face. What had Leander Mussman been thinking to even contemplate bringing his followers to this hellhole? Perhaps the man was lucky to have died. Now, at least, Gull Island would never be Mussman's bad dream. Now, Oliver reflected, Gull Island was to be his own personal nightmare. He took another painful step. That's when he saw the grave.

He couldn't be sure it was a grave. It might just be a mound of rocks. But the manner in which the mound had been assembled struck him as highly suspicious.

It would be hard to dig a grave on an island that was mostly stone. If one had to bury a body in this place it would be easier to pile rocks around it and then drag a few bits of broken greenery on top for camouflage. That's how this heap of rocks appeared to have been constructed. The vines and branches that had once disguised it were all withered or blown away.

Maybe I'm imagining things, Oliver thought. Maybe it's a mound of rocks that just happens to be roughly the length of a man. Gingerly, he approached the formation.

Despite the sweat pouring down his face and the sun's flame on his unprotected head the back of his neck felt cold. Methodically, he began dismantling the suspicious structure. An hour later he had some answers. The remains of two bodies lay beneath the rocks. Both were male and looked to have been in place for about a year. Oliver felt sure he'd solved the mysterious disappearance of tourists from Put-in-Bay. The Woodley brothers hadn't drowned or run off. They'd been murdered, more than likely by Gene Waterman.

If that supposition was correct it explained a lot. The Woodleys had been prisoners at Johnson's, but they were spearheading an encampment at Put-In-Bay that would include former prisoners from Camp Chase. Gene Rucker had changed his name to Waterman and spent half his life hiding out on Put In Bay to avoid such people. He wouldn't want his former enemies discovering his hideout by coming to Put-In-Bay on holiday.

Was he willing to do murder to discourage the Woodley's planned encampment? Apparently he was. Apparently he'd lured the Woodley brothers to Gull Island and then killed and buried them.

If it weren't for Leander Mussman's scheme reawakening interest in the island their bodies wouldn't have been discovered for decades. Rucker must have hated Mussman for his scheme to set up a community on Gull. It it had succeeded this grave would have been found and caused a sensation.

Oliver conjured up a mental image of the ghostly sailboat that had emerged from the storm and rammed Goggins' Magic Carpet. For days he'd been trying to link that event with Frank Aballo. It had seemed to make sense that Aballo would want to get rid of Hermione's fiancé.

But what if Goggins hadn't been the target? What if Pretty Girl had rammed Goggins' boat? Leander Mussman had been a passenger on the ill-fated Magic Carpet. And so was I, Oliver reflected. Waterman had reason to get rid of both of us. Mussman and I were stirring up matters that he wanted forgotten. Now he's made sure we won't be stirring up anything but flies.

Oliver replaced the rocks and staggered back to the waterfront. He stripped off his clothes and waded into the lake. The waves knocked him about but he kept going, only pausing when the water was finally over his head.

CHAPTER TWENTY-FOUR

He was trapped in an underwater cave. It's clammy stone echoed with the roar of sea monsters. Shadowy horrors crowded around him and bared their fangs.

"Oliver! Oh, for pity's sake! Oliver!"

Marietta's voice dragged him from the outlandish hallucination. Happy to be rescued from his hellish dream he stared confusedly up at her.

Her red hair hung about her face in windblown strands. Her green eyes were dark with worry. "What happened to you? My God, were you trying to drown yourself?"

"No. No, of course not."

Clad only in his wet Union suit, he was splayed on his back at the water's edge. Cold water lapped around his knees. One of his sunburned hands clutched a strand of eelgrass. It smelled of dead fish and so did he.

Embarrassed to be found in such a state, he struggled to push himself into a sitting position. It was a painful process.

"Oh, your poor leg!" Marietta exclaimed. "It's all bloody. How have you injured yourself?"

He became aware of the others. Jay Cooke, Owen Brown, Agatha and Hermione Mussman, and a woman he didn't recognize, all hovered a little distance away. Distracted by their presence and humiliated by his state, he didn't notice what Marietta was doing until he felt her hands beneath his shoulders. She was endeavoring to drag him back from the water.

"Let me do that." Owen Brown hurried forward.

"Don't! I don't need help." Oliver's inarticulate croak was entirely ignored, and rightly so. He was weak as a baby. When he tried to move his limbs felt like pudding.

Brown and Cooke carried him to a dry spot and lay him down in the shade of a tall bush. "You're a mess," he said. "That burn you've got on your face must be a misery!" He produced a flask and held Oliver's head while he trickled water down his throat. "Don't try and take too much. Easy does it."

Oliver closed his eyes. He felt Marietta's hand on his forehead. "You're feverish!" she exclaimed. "Oh Ollie, I've been so worried!"

The men bundled him into Cooke's steam launch, rigged an umbrella over his head for shade and set off for Gibralter. While the boat plowed Erie's glittering waves, Marietta sat at his side and fed him bits of bread moistened with sun tea. At first the food was almost impossible for his dry throat to swallow. Eventually he began to feel a little better.

"How did you find me?" he croaked. "Coincidence?"

"Nothing of the kind!" Marietta leaned in close and whispered, "I saw you sneak out of the hotel last night. I wondered what you were up to so I followed. I watched you sail off in that man's boat. When he came back without you I suspected something was wrong."

"Did you speak to Waterman?"

"No. I didn't like the look of him. Not one little bit. I could tell he'd been up to no good."

He stared at her. "How did you know to find me on Gull?"

"Carmen and I begged Jay Cooke to go looking for you. When I told him which direction you'd sailed in, he said it sounded as if you'd been going to Gull Island. You had told him you'd visit the place."

"That's true. He asked me to investigate its suitability for Leander's Memorial Service."

"Exactly. So when I told him I thought you might be lost there he was quite willing to help me find you."

Oliver turned his head slightly and squinted. The sun reflecting off the water was still painfully bright. "Who's that woman?"

"Carmen? Carmen Reed."

"Leander's second wife?"

"Or third. Or fourth. Who knows how many women Leander may have taken to the altar. I do know he married Carmen before he hitched himself to Agatha. That woman has no right to decide where his Memorial Service should be held."

"Will it be held on Gull Island?"

"No such thing! Carmen and Jay Cooke have agreed that Gull Island is totally inappropriate. It wouldn't be safe. Mourners might get sunstroke or be bitten by snakes."

Oliver gazed at the two Mrs. Mussmans. They sat on opposite sides of the boat, their heads averted from each other. Agatha's face was tight-lipped and stern. Carmen Reed looked equally pale and displeased. She was a small, plump woman with light brown hair blown loose from its topknot. He remembered now that he had seen her costumed as a fairy for Midsummer Night's Dream.

Though pretty, she was not beautiful enough to be a leading lady and was beginning to show her age. Lines around her eyes and mouth would soon deepen into wrinkles. There was a steely set to her mouth. It wouldn't be easy for her to go on making her living as an actress. He was glad she might inherit something from her runaway husband. On the other hand, if Leander had spent all of Agatha's money on his church how would she continue? Would she be dependent on her stepdaughter—a stepdaughter who didn't like her very much and who was in love with a train robber?

His gaze shifted to Hermione who huddled near a coil of rope. She looked miserable. He wondered if she'd heard from her outlaw lover yet. He guessed from her downcast expression that she hadn't. Why not, he asked himself. Surely now that she was an heiress she'd be more attractive to Frank Aballo than ever before.

He closed his eyes against a wave of nausea. His wounded leg throbbed in rhythm with the boat's engine. He felt sore from head to foot. A moment later he was unconscious.

When the launch arrived at Gibralter he was carried up to Owen Brown's cottage and put in the room where Leander had died. The women cleaned his wound and re-bandaged it. Marietta helped him into fresh pajamas, fed him some warm soup and put cool cloths on his smoldering forehead and neck.

Chagrined by his weakness, he thanked her for her kindness.

"You sound surprised. Did you think I wouldn't help you if you needed it?"

"I never thought about it at all."

She laughed. "Doubtless because you never expected you'd need my help. You consider yourself invincible, don't you Ollie? You always have."

"Hardly. You saved my life, Marietta. I'm grateful."

She cocked her head. "Why were you in that water? Did that man throw you overboard?"

"No. I went in myself."

"You weren't trying to drown yourself were you, Ollie?"

"No, only trying to get clean."

"Clean?"

"It's hard to explain. I felt dirty." He thought about the rocky grave with its two dead men. He considered telling Marietta what he'd discovered but quickly thought better of that.

She murmured, "Your poor, poor burned skin. Oh Oliver, what happened? How did you receive the wound on your leg? Did that man shoot you?"

"Not now," he muttered. "Just let me sleep. I need to sleep."

He dropped into unconsciousness. When he woke up Jay Cooke was sitting at his bedside.

"Well Mr. Redcastle, feeling better I hope."

"Yes sir." Oliver cleared his throat and tried again. "Yes sir, much better," he said more distinctly. "Thank you for your rescue."

"Not at all. Glad to do it. I must admit I was skeptical when Miss Dumont came to me with the story of your disappearance. But I had intended to visit Gull in any case. I'm very glad I did. That island is no place to get stranded."

"I agree."

"I was reluctant to quiz you while you were feeling so poorly. Now that you've had a rest I must know." He pointed at Oliver's wounded leg. "Someone shot you. How did it happen?"

"A private argument."

"Private? Between you and what villain?"

"Please sir, I'd rather not say until I've looked into the matter myself."

"But I must insist! To abandon an injured man on that place is tantamount to murder. What if Miss Dumont hadn't noticed you missing? You might have starved."

"I'm certain the man who left me would have had second thoughts and come back to retrieve me."

Cooke looked doubtful. "What makes you think so?"

"Because he's not a villain, only a fool and a hothead."

"You're telling me you want to settle this matter yourself?"

"I feel I must."

"You won't tell me the name of your assailant?"

"Not now, sir."

Cooke shook his head. "If you want my opinion you're making a mistake. A man who would do such a thing is dangerous. I beg you, don't do anything foolish by way of revenge."

"I won't." And that was all Oliver would say.

The next morning Cooke urged him to rest on Gibralter for another day but Oliver refused. Owen Brown lent him a clean shirt and trousers and rowed him back to Put-In-Bay. He returned to his hotel and armed himself. Then he hired a horse and turned its head in the direction of Gene Waterman's cabin.

CHAPTER TWENTY FIVE

High overhead the sun glinted through the leaves. Oliver guided his horse onto Waterman's track. The animal changed course grudgingly and halted under a tree, clearly determined to graze.

Oliver would have won the battle of wills if he'd felt less shaky. Truthfully, he was glad of the rest. Slumping in the saddle so that his throbbing head came within inches of the pommel, he closed his eyes. His skin was drum-tight and raw from sunburn and he still felt feverish.

While the animal nibbled contentedly, he lay against its neck. A ray of warmth found its way through the canopy of leaves and struck the barrel of the revolver in his belt, heating the steel pressed against his belly. He told himself he couldn't waste time like this. Nor could he make a sitting duck of himself while Waterman/Rucker might be in the neighborhood. Straightening, he pulled the horse's head out of the grass and urged it on down the lane. When he judged himself within walking distance of his quarry's cabin he left his mount tied to a tree shielded by bushes and proceeded on foot.

Not wanting to come out into the open before necessary he circled through the thick screen of greenery until he had gotten a look at the shack from three sides. It appeared uninhabited. Waterman's horse and wagon were nowhere in sight. All the better, Oliver thought. He'd be able to arrange a proper reception for his problematic colleague.

He slipped out from behind a leafy oak and made a closer inspection of the premises. The house was definitely empty. Oliver looked around, considering where he should station himself to wait. It was crucial to take Waterman by surprise. The last thing he wanted was to shoot the man. He had not come to this island to be sidetracked by a disgruntled ex-Pinkerton. He couldn't be sure that Waterman had murdered the two men he'd found on Gull. Though it seemed likely. If he had killed them and then hidden their bodies on that godforsaken wasteland he might have had good reason.

The two dead men had been former Rebs. Waterman's prison ordeal when he went undercover for Pinkerton had turned him paranoid. Even if the two dead men were blameless, Waterman could have imagined them to be prison camp foes coming after him bent on revenge. Or perhaps they had recognized him, and he'd killed them to save his skin.

The scenario was not far-fetched. Things had happened in the War Between the States that could never be forgotten or forgiven. Oliver knew only too well that he had war enemies who would like nothing better than to put a bullet through his brain. In fact, he'd had to bury a couple of them himself. He was not entirely unsympathetic to Waterman's straits.

Perhaps, Oliver speculated, Waterman had lured him to Gull Island because he feared exposure. If that were the case Waterman had miscalculated. Oliver was not interested in seeing a colleague hang because he'd killed an old war enemy in self-defense. Sometimes a man had no choice but to protect himself whatever way he could. Really, all Oliver desired was an explanation. Once he had that he'd sort out what to do.

He was heading toward a thick stand of shrubbery bordering the head of the path from the road when he spotted the cat he'd seen earlier. It lay sprawled in the grass, blood leaking from its ears where its head had been nearly severed by the blow of a large knife or possibly even an ax. Waterman at work? Looking down at the mangled body Oliver reminded himself that even if Waterman really had killed the two ex-Rebs in self-defense he was sneaky and violent and needed to be approached with care.

Nearby was the hole where Oliver had seen the animal disappear. He veered toward the spot. It was big enough for a man to get into and might be a good place to lie in wait for his murderous host.

When he lowered himself into the opening, however, he found it to be more than just a hole in the ground. It dropped some six feet and then widened. Before leaving town Oliver had equipped himself with a fresh box of matches. He struck one so he could get a better look at his subterranean surroundings. Apparently, he and the cat weren't the first to explore this place. An oil lamp sat on the dirt floor. It was three quarters full of oil and, judging from its condition, had been used recently. Oliver lit it and held it high.

Its yellow light revealed an arched channel that angled away into obscurity. Intrigued, he began to explore. He had expected the passage to end within a few feet. Instead of petering out it continued, sometimes narrowing or swinging away at an angle but always resuming a course which he judged to be roughly parallel to the water's edge.

It was well used. The dirt on the floor showed footprints that had been traced and retraced. He ran across two oil lamps set in rough niches, both at least half full of fuel. He ceased to worry about running out of light. It must be Waterman who'd placed the lamps, he thought. Obviously the man spent a lot of time down here. Why? Where did the passage lead? Perhaps finding out would answer some questions.

Oliver crawled through a narrow rock formation and then rolled over on his back so that he could examine the ceiling. It was pebbled by snot-like formations that looked unpleasantly wet to the touch, as if the very earth was ailing with a bad head cold.

He had been exploring for no more than a quarter of an hour but with every second the air seemed to thicken. Drawing breath became more of a labor. His skin felt clammy in the chill. The weight of the stone and earth above him pressed down like an executioner's heavy hand. He acknowledged to himself that he was not cut out to be a caver and considered turning around. Waterman might appear at any minute and he didn't want to lose the opportunity to take him by surprise.

He came upon a narrowing in the passage. A fence post and good size boulder lay to the right of it. Grooves under and around the boulder indicated that it may have corked up the entry at one time and someone had used the fence post to lever it away.

Oliver crawled into the bottleneck and inched a few more feet. Finally he poked his head through an opening barely wide enough to accommodate his shoulders. The moment his nose was on the other side of the stricture he noticed the freshening of the air. He inhaled deeply and thought he could smell water.

Encouraged, he moved forward, pushing the lantern ahead of him as he inched his way through the narrow stone throat. Just ahead of him the stricture widened. He used his fingertips to shove the lantern out into the opening and was abruptly plunged into darkness. A draft on the other side of the narrow had snuffed it out. Oliver cursed. He rested for a moment and hen resumed struggling. That was his only option until he was in the clear and could relight the lantern.

In the total darkness of his close confinement he felt like a blind gopher jammed into a buried pipe. Finally he managed to wriggle past the sticking point. With a grunt he heaved himself onto his knees and felt around for the lantern. He had just put a finger on its metal base when the blow struck his head.

Oliver opened his eyes. Gene Waterman stood grinning down at him. The lantern he held over his head carved deep shadows under his brows and lit the evil smirk of his mouth. "So we meet again," he said. "You got more lives than a cat, don't you Redcastle. But, as you may have noticed on your way in, I finally got the cat. It won't be a nuisance of itself no more. Now I got you."

Oliver tried to move and found that his hands and feet were tied. He was stretched full length on the stone floor of a large, low-ceilinged chamber. To his right he saw a small pool of milky looking water. On the other side of it he saw a cage large enough to accommodate a Collie-sized dog. Inside the cage, curled into what looked like an excruciating position, he saw the body of a man.

"That's right," Waterman said. "You got company. Wondering who that is? Well, let me tell you. Meet Mister Frank Aballo."

Oliver stared. "Frank Aballo?"

"The very same. All this time I've had him. What do you think of that?"

"How?"

"Caught him camping out down here without his beard."

"Beard?" Oliver repeated stupidly. He was still dazed by the blow to his head and desperately trying to come to grips with his situation.

"Meet Professor Paradise. All this time Aballo was going around the island in disguise. He'll tell you himself when he wakes up." Waterman pointed at the caged figure. "He ain't saying anything because I knocked him on the head to keep him quiet while I was laying for you."

"Amazing," Oliver muttered. He was furious with himself. How had he imagined that Waterman might have a reasonable explanation for his behavior? How had he let this evil brute bamboozle him all over again?

Waterman answered the question with obvious enjoyment. I saw you coming, Redcastle. I came down here to hide, thinking you'd like to kill me. When I heard you come on down that hole I figured I was finished. Then I thought, no, I ain't finished. I'll just wait here and take my chances." A cacophony of fiendish cackles bounced off the stone walls. "And so I did," Waterman chortled. "Here you are all trussed up like a Christmas pig. Guess you ain't so high and mighty after all." He kicked Oliver in the ribs. Then kicked him a second time for good measure.

Oliver decided not to mention the two bodies he'd discovered on Gull. Now that he knew his captor had Aballo men who had been dead for more than a year no longer seemed to be the issue. "What is it you want?" he gasped when he was able to speak.

"From you? Why nothing. You ain't worth spit to me now." He indicated the pistol which he'd removed from Oliver's belt and stuck into his own.

"What about Aballo?"

"I got what I want from him."

"The location of the train loot?"

"Exactly. You and he can stay alive down here until I make sure he told me the truth. I'm going to do that right now."

"Bastard!"

"Now, now, I ain't such a bad fella'. Why, I'll even leave a light so you won't be afraid of the dark. Oh, by the by, I searched you and took away all your knives. I just tell you that so you won't hurt yourself wriggling around trying to get at them. You're clean as a baby." Waterman set the lantern on the stone floor and began to crawl through the opening that led into the cavern. He was considerably smaller than Oliver and made it through with relative ease.

When he was on the other side he shouted, "I'm sealing you in, Redcastle. You ain't going anywhere."

A moment later Oliver heard the grating of rock on rock and knew that Waterman was rolling the stone in front of the passage. It took him a good ten minutes to accomplish the task. Finally, the mammoth stone settled against the opening with a thunderous boom.

CHAPTER TWENTY-SIX

Aballo groaned and tried to stretch his legs, an impossibility inside the tight confine of his dog cage. His knees clanged against the metal bars and the pain of the failed effort woke him up.

Light from the oil lamp still flickered over the cave's stone interior. Oliver could see the shadows Aballo's long black lashes cast as his eyelids fluttered open.

How, Oliver wondered, had he been fooled into taking this youngster for that old huckster, Professor Paradise? Either I'm thick as a board or Aballo is a mighty clever actor, he thought. Maybe both. Having been twice fooled by Waterman Oliver was beginning to doubt his own wits. Perhaps in the course of his long and violent career he'd been hit on the head once too often.

He said, "I know you by reputation, Frank. Can't say I'm happy to meet you in these particular circumstances."

Aballo squinted through the bars of his cage. He appeared even more befuddled than Oliver felt. He also looked half-starved and badly beaten. Welts, bruises and bloody wounds dotted his body. An angry burn mark scarred his cheek. Even so, Oliver could see why Hermione had fallen in love with him. Despite his battered appearance he had the dark good looks of a gypsy Adonis. He asked, "Who are you?"

"Name's Oliver Redcastle. I've been tracking you for Pinkerton's."

"Tracking me?"

"To recover the money you robbed. Unfortunately for me, I tracked you here."

"Here." Aballo took in the cave and the ropes binding Oliver's hands and feet. "That sick bastard got you, too?"

"Knocked me on the head when I crawled in here to explore."

Aballo struggled, trying to change his cramped position, and then howled in an agony of fury and rage. His scream turned into a wail of despair. "I don't give a damn who you are!" he finally choked out. "What does it matter when we're both dead men?"

"We're not dead yet."

"This is a tomb. That madman has sealed us up like beetles in a jar."

"How long have you been a prisoner here?"

"I don't know. Forever, it seems."

"By my calculation, not more than three days."

"Three days in hell is an eternity."

"How long have you been in that cage?"

"Not the whole three days, thank God! That devil dragged it down in pieces and bolted it together. Damn him to hell! He shoved me into it a few hours ago. At least, I think it was a few hours ago. Time doesn't mean much in this place."

Gradually Oliver drew the story out of him. Disguised as Professor Paradise, Aballo had set himself up with the diving horse concession and then waited for the Mussmans to show up on the island.

Louise Titchener

"This was all so you could get in touch with Hermione?"

"I knew that witch of a stepmother wouldn't let me anywhere near her. I had to disguise myself so she wouldn't recognize me."

"Mighty resourceful of you. How did you manage to set up here with no help. Or did someone on the island help you out?"

"I did it on my own," Aballo declared.

But Oliver wondered. Did Aballo have a contact on the island who'd given him aid and comfort? That might explain the success of his masquerade. It wouldn't be easy to pull off such a complicated charade otherwise.

He said, "Surely you understand why the Mussmans didn't fancy having you hanging around their daughter."

"They made it plain they don't think I'm good enough for her."

"But you think you are."

"I know I'm not. That doesn't stop me from being in love with her."

"Love," Oliver muttered as he began to slither along the stone floor."

"What are you doing?" Aballo asked.

"I want to get close to you before the light dies. Maybe we can help each other out. Maybe you can untie me and I can get your cage unlocked."

"I doubt it."

"It's worth a try. You've escaped from prisons before."

"Yes, when I had the right equipment and a lucky break. I don't see anything like that now."

200

"Maybe something will turn up." Oliver eyed the distance between himself and Aballo's cage. With his arms and legs so tightly bound it would be agonizing to close it before the oil in the lantern gave out.

Aballo watched in silence as he wriggled like a crippled snake around the perimeter of the pool, a good twelve feet across. When Oliver was half way around he commented, "I'm glad Hermione doesn't know I'm down here. It would kill her to know I was in such a fix."

"You believe the girl is in love with you, then."

"I know she is. It's always been her family that stood between us. It's not my fault we fell in love. When I came to the mission I only wanted a meal. Then I saw her." He closed his eyes. "She's wonderful, beautiful! I'll be in love with her until I die! I'd do anything to make her my wife."

"How did you think that might happen? You're a wanted man. You were a fool to rob that train."

"I was a wanted man before I met Hermione, and nothing can change the fact of that. I robbed the train because I had nothing to lose and something to gain."

"What did you have to gain besides the money?" When Aballo didn't answer Oliver said, "Let me see if I can guess." He rolled over on his back to rest and nearly tipped into the pool. Saving himself just barely, he said, "You planned to take the money across the border and persuade Hermione to join you there. You thought if you could tempt her with a stolen fortune she'd be willing to cast off her family."

The young man's handsome face turned sulky. He kept silent but his expression was all the answer Oliver required.

"I've guessed right, haven't I? You and Hermione were planning to run off to Canada. Or, at least, you were trying to persuade her to elope with you against her parents' wishes. Were you successful?"

"I've already told you, Hermione is in love with me."

"I don't doubt it. You're a handsome devil and she's an impressionable young girl." Oliver had resumed his struggle and was half way around the pool now. "But perhaps," he grunted as he inched along, "she had her doubts. You're an outlaw and she was engaged to a rich and respectable man."

Aballo snapped, "Maybe I wasn't good enough for her but neither was that fat fool her father forced on her!"

"So you killed Goggins to get him out of the way and make her easier to persuade?"

"What?" Aballo looked shocked. "I didn't kill Gabriel Goggins. He drowned."

"He drowned after a rogue sailboat crashed into his canoe. I should know. I was in the canoe and so was her father."

"You're crazy."

"You were there on Middle Bass that night. I saw you with Hermione. Perhaps you and she planned to make sure that Gabriel would be lost in the storm you saw blowing up."

"I may be a robber but I'm no killer. And Hermione is an angel. She wouldn't plan to murder anyone and she certainly wouldn't scheme to tip her father into a stormy lake."

"Yet you and she both benefit greatly from his and Goggins' deaths. Now she's an heiress and free to marry anyone she chooses."

"I'm no saint but I'm not a murderer, either. Hermione would never marry me if she thought I arranged to drown her father and her fiancé. Yes, I was jealous of Goggins. But I didn't kill him."

Oliver believed Aballo was telling the truth. Did that mean his original theory about Waterman was correct? Had he engineered the accident to get rid of Mussman so that the bodies buried on Gull Island wouldn't be found.

CHAPTER TWENTY SEVEN

As Oliver continued struggling toward Aballo's cage the young man described how he'd been captured by Gene Waterman.

"I heard about the island's network of caves. At first I set up in a cave across from Perry's Cave. But I soon realized that wouldn't work. Too many people knew about the place."

Oliver nodded. That explained the blanket and empty cans he'd seen when he was with Brown and Venator.

Aballo continued, "I explored the coastline hoping to find a safe hideout. I couldn't stay in character twenty-four hours a day. I needed a place where I could dump my disguise and get some rest."

He'd found Waterman's cave by accident. While camping rough in the woods nearby he'd seen the cat disappear down a hole and followed.

"When I crawled into this place I thought I'd hit pay-dirt," he said glumly.

"Gene Waterman surprised you down here?"

Aballo grimaced. "I was asleep. Dead to the world. He snapped handcuffs to my hands and feet, and I was done for."

"Then what?"

"He hung me up on a hook and tortured me."

"Tortured?"

"No other word for it. He lit a candle and held it under my feet. He took off his belt and beat me with it. You can see the blood caked on my shirt."

Oliver nodded.

"He wanted the train money, and he wasn't about to take no for an answer."

"I gather you didn't have your loot with you down here."

"I'm not crazy. It's hidden where it won't be found."

"And our friend wanted to know where."

"In the worst way!"

"You told him?"

Aballo groaned. "Eventually. It was either that or have my toes burnt off."

The oil lamp's yellow glow was weakening when Oliver finally managed to slither alongside the cage. He pivoted to angle his boots close to the young man's hands.

"Why are you showing me your feet?"

"There's a blade hidden in my left heel."

Aballo's expression brightened. "And that evil bastard never found it. Clever of you!"

"If you can cut the ropes on my hands before the light dies I can take care of the rest." Oliver thought he could pick the lock on the cage--so long as the oil lamp stayed lit.

It took some time to extract the small blade from its hiding place. Sticking his arms out between the bars at an awkward angle, Aballo set to work sawing the ropes. They were thick and refused to give way easily.

"Ouch!" Oliver said when the knife bit into his wrist.

"Sorry. I'm so twisted up in here I can barely move. It'll be wonderful to get free and stretch my legs."

"Can you walk with those burned feet?"

"I don't know. Maybe it doesn't matter. We're jailed in a stone strongbox and no way to get out."

"If Waterman doesn't come back we'll have to figure a way to move that rock he's pushed up against the entrance." Oliver wondered if this could be done. The passage leading to the massive rock corking them in was so constricted there would be no way to get any leverage against it. At least, none he could think of at the moment.

"Oh, he's coming back," Aballo said.

"How can you be sure?"

"He tortured me until I'd had enough. I told him where the train loot was buried."

"Yes. You already said that."

"I told him it was on Middle Bass."

"And?"

"I lied. He's on a wild goose chase. When he figures that out there'll be hell to pay. He'll probably kill us both."

Oliver took a deep breath. "More likely he'll shoot me and cut you to pieces until you've given him what he wants. Then he'll kill you, too."

Aballo redoubled his efforts and the frayed strands of rope finally parted. Oliver took the blade and set to work on his feet. When they were free he turned his attention to the lock on the cage. It was simple enough, and he could use the smaller end of the blade to work it. The light flickered and died.

For a long moment the two men were silent, overcome by the weight of darkness that had descended upon them. Aballo cursed. Oliver said nothing, too busy re-orienting himself to the changed conditions to put his rushing thoughts into words. He pressed his fingertips to the cage's cold metal.

"Can you crack it in the dark?" the confined man hissed.

"I'll have to try. Quiet. This is going to take some focus."

The cave was so silent that Oliver could hear the blood pulsing through his veins. Or was that the rush and retreat of the lake beating against their rocky enclosure? He decided it must be Lake Erie, which meant that the lake was close.

Now that his pupils had adjusted the cave didn't appear quite so pitch black. A phosphorescent glow came off the underground pond, giving it the look of a ghostly eye. The lake water seeping through the rocks would have absorbed phosphorous along with other minerals. How far had it traveled, he wondered? Had the milky water collected in the pond been absorbed by a layer of rock resembling a sponge? Or had it come up through a conduit large enough to accommodate a man's body?

Remembering his last attempt to swim into a cave, Oliver shuddered. He had a vivid sense of how it would be to get stuck in an underground passage and drown. Pushing the horrible image from his mind's eye, he concentrated on the cage.

It took ten minutes of fumbling and cursing to get its lock undone.

"If I were on your side of the bars I'd have had it open by now," Aballo complained at one point.

"Well, you're the bank robber, not me."

The lock clicked open. Oliver yanked at the tiny door and dragged Aballo through it. When he was finally freed he lay groaning on the stone floor.

"Can you move?"

"My legs are dead."

"Try."

"I'm trying. I can't even feel my feet! If I could I'd probably be screaming!"

"We have to be ready for Waterman. He could come back any time now."

"What can we do against him? He'll be armed to the teeth."

"True, but he has to roll that stone away and then crawl through the bottleneck. He laid a trap. So can we."

CHAPTER TWENTY EIGHT

They'd had no more than half an hour to prepare when they heard stone scrape against stone.

"That's him," Aballo whispered. "He's prying that rock loose."

Oliver pictured Waterman manhandling the fence post to maneuver the boulder away from the opening. He whispered, "It's going to take a while. We've got a few more minutes."

"I'll be ready." Still crippled, Aballo knelt to one side of the entrance to the inner cave. Their jailer would have to crawl through the narrow cavity, making him vulnerable to attack. The young man was armed with a skull-sized rock.

Opposite Aballo, Oliver prepared to tackle their jailer. He rubbed his thumb over the miniature blade he'd had hidden in the heel of his boot.

The crash and boom of Waterman's labor reverberated in their stone prison. A weak thread of light pierced the clammy darkness.

"You two still in there?" Waterman panted.

The waiting men kept silent. Let their tormenter think they'd passed out in fright.

"Not talking? You can't fool me. I know you ain't gone nowhere. Mighty cute, Frank, sending me off on a wild goose chase. Skeeters bit me up bad while I was pokin' around where you said you'd hid the money. Got my feelings hurt when I realized you'd lied to me. Here I thought we was friends. Guess I was mistaken."

Waterman's breathing had evened out, and his voice sounded deceptively mild. Yet, Oliver could feel the rage churning beneath the surface. The muscles in his legs tightened.

"Still not talking? You'd like me to think nobody's to home in that cave. Won't work! I know you're both there 'cause there's no way you could get out."

He paused, waiting. Still Oliver and Aballo held their tongues.

"On the other hand, after I left you I got to thinking about our mutual friend, Mr. Redcastle. Mighty clever fellow, Mr. Oliver Redcastle. In the old days he had a rep for carrying more than one weapon. Sometimes even strapped a knife to his leg or hid one in his boot. When I searched him I forgot about the boot. What if he got himself loose?"

Light flared and Oliver was momentarily blinded. A burning object shot through the entry past his feet. Waterman had pitched a kerosene-soaked wick fashioned into a ball. It lit up the cave. If he were crouched at the opening, where he'd no doubt positioned himself, he would see that Aballo's cage was empty.

The flaming ball rolled into the water in front of the cage and sputtered out. But it had stayed alight long enough to tell the story.

Darkness descended over the cave and Waterman said, "Well, well, well. So you two are loose in there. Planning to do me a mischief? Well I ain't planning to allow that, and I ain't playing no more games, neither. Frank, you got two choices. Either crawl out here and tell me where you hid that money, or stay put and be damned. You listenin'?"

Aballo said, "What about Redcastle?"

"What about him?"

"If he comes out will you kill him?"

"I ain't talking to Redcastle. I'm talking to you. Man can do what he pleases, stay or come out. But if Redcastle stays and you keep him company you're a dead man. That's certain. If you're not out by the time I count to ten I'm going to roll this stone back into place and drop a stick of dynamite down here."

Waterman began counting. His two captives stared at each other. In the gloom Oliver could only make out Aballo's outline. Even so, his tense body language was clear. Without a word the younger man dropped onto all fours and began wriggling toward the light.

As his heels disappeared into the narrow neck of stone, Oliver sank onto his haunches. He listened to Waterman crow with triumph as he pulled Aballo through to the other side. He heard the click of handcuffs snapping onto Aballo's wrists. Then he heard the ominous grating of stone.

"Goodbye Ollie," Waterman whispered just before the boulder settled back into place. "Say hello to Allan Pinkerton when you see him in hell."

The stone sealed the cave and plunged Oliver into blackness so profound that he almost felt as if he didn't exist. He squeezed his eyelids shut and listened to the harsh rasp of his own breathing. He shivered with cold. Nausea spread through his guts.

Waterman wouldn't come back. I'm going to die here, Oliver thought. Already he felt weak. In a few days without food or drinkable water he'd be helpless. Perhaps years from now his bones would be found. People would wonder how he'd come to be corked up like a cockroach in a bottle, but no one would have the answer. It would be one of those amusing island riddles people discussed over beer and ice cream.

He opened his eyes and turned his head toward a dim glow. The phosphorous in the pool of water shimmered faintly, seeming to beckon him. Slowly he got to his feet, walked over to it and looked down. There seemed no bottom to the milky water. Yet it must connect with the lake somewhere. Oliver took a deep breath and dived in.

CHAPTER TWENTY-NINE

Oliver floated on a streak of silver moonlight. He gulped deep, silky breaths of night air. The lake was warm, like bath water, and in the darkness he felt strangely safe.

He was too weak to think of finding the shore. His strength had been drained in the struggle to swim through the underwater passage linking Waterman's cave with Lake Erie.

He'd plunged into the cave's milky pool expecting to die there. Drowning had seemed preferable to slow starvation. He'd had only the slimmest of hopes that the pool would provide an escape. Yet that's what it had granted.

Seconds after he'd hit the water he'd kicked his way into a level passage. Assuming that he would be entombed in the underwater channel, he'd propelled himself forward. Instead of narrowing, as he'd feared, the channel had widened. Though blinded by the inky water, he'd been able to swim freely.

Still, long before he came to the end of it he'd run out of air. How he had managed to make it out to the lake and rise to the surface he would never be able to explain. All he knew now was the sweetness of air in his aching lungs.

He would have slipped back into unconsciousness if something hadn't brushed up against his legs, either a fish or a water snake. Startled, he put his feet down and touched bottom. A few minutes later he crawled up on a stony beach.

Moonlight etched the profile of a massive boulder. It squatted like a granite hen in a nest of smaller egg-shaped stones. Oliver knew where he was. When he'd first arrived on the island he had gone swimming on this beach and noticed this distinctive rock formation. So he'd washed up on Waterman's property. What's more, he could look up and see a dim yellow light leaking under the man's closed door.

With his eyes fixed on Waterman's cabin, Oliver climbed the steep slope. His bare feet slipped and slid in the grassy weeds. Hungry mosquitoes buzzed around his head. Batting them away, he advanced to within fifty yards of the structure, then knelt in a patch of saw-grass to reconnoiter.

Waterman might be cutting Aballo's throat at this very moment. Oliver told himself that he had to rescue the young bank-robber quickly. How to do that without getting himself killed? It would be a lot easier if he had a gun. But he had no gun, or any other kind of weapon as the knife he'd carried in his boot was long gone.

A footstep rustled at his back. He jerked around.

"Oliver, is that you?" Marietta's voice came at him in a harsh whisper. She put a fingertip on his shoulder. "It is you. Why are you wet? What's happened?"

She was standing within a foot of him and she wasn't alone. Just behind her he made out Carmen Reed in the shadows. It was an indication of his exhaustion and disorientation that he hadn't heard their approach. Making this strange night even stranger, moonlight revealed the fact that both women were dressed in their gauzy Shakespearian costumes. It was as if fairies from Midsummer Night's Dream had come flitting out of the trees.

He hissed, "What are you doing here?"

"Looking for you. What else? After the play I checked your room. When you weren't there I decided to find you."

"Why?"

"Why do you think?" she shot back in an acid tone. "You're the father of my daughter. If you are killed by some madman Chloe will have only me. And as you've pointed out so often, I'm not much of a mother."

"I meant why here?"

"Really, Oliver, I'm not a fool. Gene Waterman lives here. I can tell there's bad blood between the two of you. I was afraid you'd come to his cabin to settle a score and he'd hurt you."

"Did you think you could rescue me from a villain dressed in that get-up?"

"I thought the two of us might. You'll notice I didn't come out here alone." She indicated Carmen. "And what does my costume have to do with anything? When I realized you were in trouble I decided not to waste time changing clothes."

"I'm flattered."

Still standing a little distance away, Carmen chuckled. "You should be, Mr. Redcastle. I told her this fairy costume wasn't the best outfit for a midnight ramble, but she insisted we hadn't a moment to lose."

On the boat coming back from Gull island Marietta's companion had been quiet. Now, however, she had a confident air. Though she was not a tall woman, her voice was deep and rich—the kind that would carry on a stage and make an impression. He could see why Leander had been attracted to her.

Marietta knelt beside Oliver. "What's happened? Are you all right?"

"It's a long story."

"You're hurt, aren't you?" She tugged on his arm. "Come back to town with me. I left a horse and buggy out on the main road."

"I can't. Waterman's up there in that cottage with a young man he may be murdering as we speak."

"What are you talking about?"

After Oliver provided a brief explanation Marietta hissed, "But that's crazy. You're weak as a kitten and he's probably got a gun."

"Probably." Oliver shook off her hand and started to crawl forward.

She grabbed his arm again. "You are the most stubborn man! Here, take this." She thrust steel into his hand. Moonlight glinted off the barrel of a small, pearl handled revolver.

"Whose gun is this?"

"Mine, of course."

"You carry a gun?"

"A woman alone needs to protect herself."

He checked to see if the weapon was loaded. It was. "Thanks," he said. "Stay put until I come back."

CHAPTER THIRTY

The wind through the tops of the trees, the slap of waves at the lake's rough edge, the incessant buzz of insects—all these had muffled the low drone coming from the cabin. Oliver was within ten feet of the door before he was able to pick out the guttural croon of Waterman's voice.

Periodically a word would emerge from the shapeless background noise and explode like a gunshot. "Bastard. . .How'd you like that?"

Oliver crept up to the grimy bit of glass that served as one of the cabin's few windows. He took several seconds to make sense of what he saw.

Frank Aballo's wrists had been bound and the rope binding them attached to an iron hook embedded in a ceiling beam. Stripped naked from the waist up, he dangled with his bare feet several inches off the packed dirt floor.

His lean back dripped blood and so did his feet. Waterman, cracked a leather belt at them. Flinching uselessly, Aballo howled "Stop!"

"Tell me where it's at! Then I'll stop!"

Aballo didn't answer.

Waterman screamed, "You gonna' make me kill you? I'll kill you if you don't tell. Don't think for a minute I won't!" He dropped the belt and snatched a butcher knife off the bunk. "I gonna' cut your damn toes off one by one. And when I'm done I'm gonna' let you bleed to death like a stuck pig!"

Oliver took a firm hold on his gun and stepped toward the cabin door. He had his hand on the bit of frayed rope that served as a door pull when he heard Aballo's voice.

"All right, all right! I'll tell you."

Oliver returned to the window.

"You going to spit out the truth this time?" Waterman demanded. "I'm warning you, boy, you lie again and I'll slit your belly up and down."

"The truth," Aballo gasped. "The truth, I swear."

"You better not be foolin' me this time."

"I'm not."

Waterman ran the edge of his knife along the surface of Aballo's quivering abdomen. "Where is it?"

"Cut me down."

"The hell I will. Spill your guts now or I'll spill 'em for you."

"I can't tell you. It's impossible!"

"Why is that?"

"Because I have to show you. You'll never find it if I don't show you."

Waterman stood with his lips curled back from his snaggled teeth, oily wisps of hair straggling down the back of his neck. The flat of his long blade rested ominously on Aballo's bare belly. Oliver took aim, ready to shoot. Then Waterman shrugged, dragged a stool across the room, climbed onto it and cut Aballo down.

"You better not be trying to fool me this time."

The boy fell in a bloody heap on the filthy floor. "I'm not, I'm not!"

"All right then, lead me to it and make it quick."

* * *

It took some time before Waterman and Frank Aballo left the cabin. The young man, crippled by his injuries, had to be dragged through the door. Outside his captor tied him to a tree and then went to hitch up his horse and wagon. Oliver stayed in the shadows listening to Aballo moan and waiting to see what would happen next.

Squinting into the darkness, he looked for Marietta and Carmen but saw no sign of them. Had the two women left or were they still in the trees observing all this? Wherever they were, he hoped they wouldn't interfere.

Waterman returned with his horse and wagon. Once he and his prisoner set off in it, Oliver followed. Keeping to the shadows so he wouldn't be seen, he was at too great a distance to hear what instructions Aballo might be giving his captor.

Fortunately, Waterman's horse plodded down the dark road at a leisurely pace. Oliver had no trouble keeping up. His exhaustion seemed to have been wiped away. All his attention was focused on the task ahead.

The wagon had proceeded about a quarter of a mile when it turned off the road onto a track. It was no more than a narrow footpath, all but invisible in the darkness.

Finally the trail emerged from the trees. Cautiously Oliver peered out from behind a spiky, vine-covered bush and surveyed the clearing ahead. Moonlight picked out the wagon. Waterman had dragged Aballo down from it and dropped him on a half circle of long grass. While the horse munched contentedly, he grabbed the young man by the scruff of the neck and shook him like a bag of marbles.

"Where'd you hide it! Tell me or I'll kill you here and now!"

CHAPTER THIRTY-ONE

"Stop! I'll tell! Just give me a chance!"

Waterman halted his rain of blows. Fists clenched, he stepped back from Aballo. "Are we in the right spot?"

"I think so."

"Think so? Son, I'm warning you. You better know so!"

"I do. I do. It's just everything looks different in the dark."

Waterman seized the young man's arm and dragged him to his feet. "Show me!"

"I can't walk."

"Then crawl, damn you! I don't care how you do it! Show me where you've hid that damned railroad money."

Aballo took a few halting steps. Looking around with an air of desperate uncertainty, he pointed at a cluster of scraggly bushes. They clung to a patch of dirt on a flat stretch of limestone shelf overlooking the lake.

"In them bushes?" Waterman demanded.

"Twenty paces to the right."

"Twenty paces? Where'd you get that nonsense? Some fool pirate yarn? How long is a damned pace?"

"The longest step I could take."

"Then start steppin'!"

Aballo yelped, "You've crippled me! How can I take long steps when I can barely walk at all?"

Oliver slipped out into the open. Keeping close to the ground, he skirted the moonlit area where the two men were squabbling and crept down past them to a stand of trees near the bit of earth where he conjectured they were headed.

Concealed in the shelter of two hackberries he watched as Waterman dragged a reluctant Aballo down the rocky incline toward the bushes. Oliver strained to hear what they were saying but the rising wind blew away Aballo's complaints and Waterman's curses.

Oliver closed his eyes and for a brief instant felt almost at peace. It was strange, considering that in a few minutes he planned to attack Waterman. He'd had that same experience many times before going into combat. Some might call it the calm before the storm. He thought of it as a kind of centering, an interval of clarity before the ultimate confusion. The moment had always held a perverse pleasure.

As captive and jailer drew near the bushes Oliver began to pick up faint snatches of their continuing argument.

"I'll try."

"You'd best do better than try!"

"But I can't walk. I'll have to crawl."

"Then crawl, wriggle on your belly like a damn snake for all I care!"

Waterman let go and Aballo collapsed into a boneless heap. He lay on the ground, his moans blending with the sigh of the rising wind. He flinched away ineffectually when Waterman delivered a mean kick to his ribs.

"Get going!"

Aballo heaved himself up onto all fours and began heading toward the stand of trees where Oliver was hidden. He drew back into their shelter. When Aballo gained the edge of the tree-line, he paused and felt about on the ground with his palms and fingertips.

"What you doing?" Waterman demanded.

"It's here somewhere. The dirt ought to be loose where I buried it."

"Get outa' my way!" Waterman shoved Aballo, sending him sprawling. Ignoring the young man's yelp of pain, he dropped onto his own hands and knees. Careless of his injured prisoner he began to scrabble about in the dirt.

"It's here," he crowed. "I can feel it." He clawed at the ground.

Aballo sprang to his feet. He seized a fallen branch and whacked his foe's head so hard that the crack of wood against skull cut through the wind like a bullet.

Oliver watched this in amazement. He, like Waterman, had been convinced that the young man was too badly injured to be any threat. Not so. Aballo hopped lithely from foot to foot, shouting curses and whirling the branch around his head like a battle axe.

The first blow had flattened Waterman so that he lay with his face in the dirt. When he made to roll over Aballo whacked him again and wound up to put all his strength into another strike. Oliver threw himself at the boy. Taken by surprise, Aballo staggered and fell on his back. Oliver pinned him to the ground and wrestled the club away.

The young man regained his wits and, with the agility of a desperate acrobat, fought back. He was strong and double-jointed. Nor did he fight fair. He bit and kicked, using his elbows and knees to deliver sharp jabs. Oliver had his work cut out to subdue him. They rolled across the ground like spitting cats.

At last Oliver was able to use his superior weight and strength to overcome his younger, more agile adversary. Holding both Aballo's wrists flat to the ground, he planted a knee in his belly and stared into his twisted face.

"Why did you stop me?" Aballo panted.

"What did you plan on doing? Did you want to kill the man?"

"He would have killed me."

Oliver glanced at Waterman, who lay motionless, perhaps dead already. He glared at Aballo. "You've already got robbery on your plate. Don't be a young fool! Do you want to be hung for murder as well?"

"It wouldn't be murder, only self-defense."

"Good luck convincing a judge. Once the man was down to strike him again would have been murder. I'd testify to that myself."

"What do you care? He would have killed you. I thought he already had."

"I'm not so easy to kill."

"So I see. What now? What do you want?"

"What I've always wanted." Oliver pulled Aballo into a sitting position, twisted his arms behind his back and used his suspenders to bind the boy's wrists. He stepped back warily. "Where's the money?"

"Where do you think?" He pointed his chin at the hole Waterman had just clawed open.

CHAPTER THIRTY- TWO

It was only a few minutes work to unearth the large black leather pouch already partially uncovered. Oliver unbuckled it, revealing packs of bundled notes. The bag was stuffed with bills and small but chunky sacks of coin and other valuables.

He turned to Aballo. "Is it all there?"

The young man answered sulkily. "Everything but what it cost me to set up as Professor Paradise."

"Where'd you get the diving horse?"

"Why do you want to know?"

"Curiosity."

"You're about to take my money. Why should I satisfy your curiosity?"

"Don't then."

Aballo shrugged. "Oh, what does it matter now? An old circus friend was looking to retire and move south. I decided to take over his act."

"And bring it to the island as a disguise so you could get close to Hermione."

"Exactly."

"It worked." Oliver continued poking through the bag. As far as he could tell it contained most of the money the train company was looking to recover. He closed the container up and added, "You're slick, Frank. You were hawking your bill of goods under my nose and I never guessed you were anything but an old quack misusing a broken down horse. Animal is okay, by the way."

"Glad to hear it. What now?"

"I return the money."

"Then you're a damned fool! What about me?"

"Turn you in, too."

Aballo got up on his knees. "Listen to reason, Redcastle. Let me go. We'll split the loot and nobody will be the wiser."

"Nobody? What about our friend over there?"

They both looked at the supine figure on the ground. Before digging up the buried money Oliver had checked his pulse. Waterman was alive and hadn't appeared to be losing blood. Yet he had remained inert for almost a half hour now. Either he needed medical attention or he was playing possum.

In case it was the latter Oliver approached him gingerly.

"Throw the damned villain over the cliff and be done with him," Aballo advised. "That's what the lowdown snake deserves."

Oliver glanced over his shoulder at his baby-faced captive. "I took you for a thief but not a cold blooded killer."

"I'm not a violent man. Just practical. Ridding the world of that filthy bastard would be doing it a favor. What do you say? Chuck him off the cliff and let me go. We'll both be rich."

Oliver shook his head. "I've done a lot of things I'm not proud of. But so far I've stayed on the right side of the law. Think I'll keep it that way."

"Nobody gets hurt but the train company."

"People always get hurt when money goes missing."

Aballo made a disgusted noise. "You talk like a religious man."

"I haven't been to church in years. Religion isn't why I can't take you up on your proposition. I've been a lawman too long to cross that line."

Sensing movement Oliver snapped his head around in time to see Waterman heave a rock at his head. He dodged and the missile missed his forehead but clipped his ear. Bellowing, Waterman lunged. His hands clamped around Oliver's throat. A moment later the two men rolled across the rough ground.

Oliver fought to pry Waterman's hands loose from his throat. In the midst of their struggle, Waterman grunted, then froze like a man who'd been impaled on a spear. All the fight went out of him. He sagged onto Oliver's prone body like a felled sheep.

It took a moment for Oliver to realize that the skirmish was ended. He stared at the top of Waterman's bald head and then rolled out from under him and sat up.

Aballo asked, "What happened?"

"I don't know. I think he either fainted or died."

A female voice said, "Really? How interesting. I suggest you take his pulse and find out which it is."

Startled, Oliver turned and found himself looking down the barrel of a gun. The person holding it was Carmen Reed, and she wasn't alone. Marietta stood just behind her. Hermione knelt behind Frank Aballo, untying his bonds. In a moment she'd freed him and the two stood and embraced.

Aballo wrapped his hand around Hermione's slim waist and looked down at Oliver. "Guess the tables are turned again," he said with a broad grin.

CHAPTER THIRTY THREE

Five minutes later Oliver dropped Waterman's lifeless wrist. "He's dead."

"You killed him?" Carmen asked the question almost conversationally.

"I didn't kill Gene Waterman. How long have you been hiding in the shadows?"

"Long enough to see you dig up Frank's money and then scuffle with that ruffian."

"It's not Frank Aballo's money. As far as Waterman is concerned, I was only defending myself. He was trying to throttle me when he went limp. He must have had a heart attack."

Oliver observed that the weapon she kept pointed at him was the same Marietta had handed over earlier for his protection. Apparently, it had fallen to the ground during his struggles and Carmen had retrieved it. It didn't look as if she meant to give it up.

Marietta blurted, "Oh Carmen, we didn't see Ollie kill the man. The horrible brute must have died of natural causes."

"Perhaps."

"What does it matter? You don't care how he died."

"Of course not. I don't care a scrap how pathetic man died. It's just a question of what should be done with the body."

Oliver, still on his knees beside the cooling corpse, made a move to get to his feet. A bullet from Carmen's gun kicked up dust next to his heel. Deafened, he sank back onto his haunches.

Carmen ignored Marietta's shriek of distress. Keeping her eyes glued to Oliver, she said, "Stay put, Mr. Redcastle. I know how to shoot. In case you're wondering, I don't want to permanently maim you, but I can do it if you force me."

He looked at Marietta. "What the hell is going on here?"

"Do as Carmen says, Oliver. She's only trying to help her daughter."

"Her daughter?"

"Hermione is Carmen's daughter. I didn't tell you because I'd promised to keep it a secret."

"I should have known! Once again you've been lying to me!"

"Not really. I said Carmen and Leander were married. That was true."

"Married when?"

Carmen interrupted impatiently. "The date is of no consequence. Not that it's any of your business, our brief union produced a child. I couldn't keep the baby so Leander left the child with his aunt."

Hermione, who'd been huddling in the shelter of Aballo's arms suddenly exclaimed, "You can't be any more surprised than I was, Mister Redcastle. Until just a few weeks ago I never even dreamed that my mother was still alive."

Her accusatory tone seemed to rattle Carmen. She exclaimed, "Leander claimed you were happy with his relative. He begged me not to contact you, and I let him persuade me. I know now that it was a mistake, but at the time it seemed—reasonable."

Hermione said, "Reasonable to abandon a helpless little baby? To never see me, your own flesh and blood?"

"What else could I do? I had no way to take care of you. You were better off with Leander's mother. Then, when you were older, it was too late. But I never stopped thinking of you. When I read about the train robbery and your involvement with the thief I knew I had to help you! That's when I decided to write to you."

Hermione turned her face away and began weeping into Aballo's chest. He tightened his arms around her.

Oliver glared at Marietta. "Everything you've said to me has been a damned lie! All this time you've been in cahoots with Aballo. While you were offering to help me catch him you were scheming to get your hands on the money he stole."

She glared back. "No such thing! I came here to help an old friend whose daughter was in trouble. I never dreamed I'd run into you."

"I'm sure you didn't."

"Well it's true, Ollie. You always think the worst of me, but I'm only doing a good deed. It would kill Hermione to see the man she loves rot in prison. And why should he? It's not as if he did anything so terrible."

"Frank Aballo robbed a train. The man is a thief."

Marietta shrugged. "He promises he won't do it again. Don't you Frank?"

Aballo was too busy comforting his weeping lover to reply to Marietta's question. "Hermione," he whispered into the girl's pale hair, "I only did it because I thought I'd lost you. Without you I'd lost the will to live. You're all I want in the world. You must believe that!"

"Oh I do," she whispered between soft hiccups. "And you're all I want, Frank. You're all I've ever wanted!"

"You see?" Marietta said. "They love each other. Carmen and I are here to make sure they have a chance for happiness."

"You expect me to believe that hogwash?"

Carmen said, "After all these years of neglecting my daughter the least I can do is help her find happiness."

"Happiness with a bank robber?"

"If that's what she wants. Considering the life I've led, I'm not one to be unforgiving about mistakes. I only hope that Hermione will come to forgive me."

The girl had stopped weeping. Still clasped in the crook of her lover's arm, she declared, "I do forgive you, Mother." She looked up at Aballo. "It's time for us to go."

He nodded and, hand in hand, the pair slipped away into the darkness.

Oliver demanded, "Where are they going?"

"To a safe place. To a place where they can start a new life together."

"I suppose you mean Canada."

"I don't propose telling you the plans I've made for my child's happiness, Mr. Redcastle."

"Do you propose promoting Hermione's love match by using that gun on me?"

"Not unless you make it necessary."

He decided to test her. He jumped to his feet and lunged. A shot deafened him, muffling Marietta's scream. A split second later he found himself sprawled face down in the dirt, a stinging pain in his ankle.

"That was very foolish," Carmen said.

"My god, you've crippled me! What next? Are you going to kill me?"

"I have an alternative, Mr. Redcastle, a much pleasanter one."

He rolled over in time to see Marietta place a small bottle on the ground a foot away from him.

"What that? Poison?"

"Not at all," Carmen said. It's merely a sleeping draught."

"A likely story. What about Agatha? She'll raise hell when she realizes you've let Hermione go off with Aballo."

"I think not. Agatha and I have come to an accommodation. I won't challenge her right to handle Hermione's inheritance until her majority. In return, she'll see that Hermione is well provided for until she reaches twenty-one, and she won't interfere in her life."

"Very nice. You've thought of everything."

"Perhaps not everything, but In Agatha's case I do hold the trump card. I can prove Leander and I were married long before he married her. Now, stop trying to distract me, Mr. Redcastle. Drink what's in that bottle, and when you wake up we'll all be gone."

"Along with the money."

"Why should we take the money? Hermione has her own fortune now. You can turn the train money back to the authorities. That's all they really want. They'll stop looking for Frank when they have it."

"Why should I believe you?"

Marietta exclaimed, "Oh Ollie, don't be foolish. That's my own sleeping potion. I always have it by me when I travel. Just drink it down and everything will be all right."

"What kind of fool do you take me for?"

Marietta threw up her hands! "A pigheaded fool! A stubborn idiot who never knows what's good for him!"

Carmen interjected grimly, "If you don't drink the contents of that bottle by the time I count to ten I will shoot you in the arm. If you still refuse I will shoot you in the leg. After that I'll aim for more sensitive parts."

Oliver believed her. What's more, in all likelihood she would never be caught. Tomorrow Carmen and Marietta would leave the island with their theater company. Eventually the islanders would find his remains next to Waterman's along with the discarded gun. They would assume they'd killed each other in a drunken brawl.

While he listened to Carmen count off the numbers his accusing gaze burned into Marietta.

"Drink it," she mouthed. "Oh please, Ollie! I promise you won't be sorry."

When Carmen reached the number nine he uncorked the bottle and swallowed the murky liquid it contained.

EPILOGUE

Two days later Oliver stepped off the steamship R.B. Hayes and onto the mainland. He found a cab, directed it to the train station and purchased a ticket for Baltimore. Then he sat down to wait for his appointment.

He had not finished perusing the Cleveland newspaper when two men wearing bowler hats sat down on either side of him. "It's been a while," the one on the right said.

Oliver recognized Bill Hass, an agent he'd worked with on a bank job out west. The other man, who Hass introduced as Boyd Capilano, was a stranger to him.

Hass indicated the leather satchel between Oliver's feet. "That the goods?"

"All but five thousand. Aballo spent that much before I caught up with him."

Capilano asked, "How'd you let him get away to Canada with his lady friend?"

"Long story. If William wants to go after them, he'll have to find another hound dog. I'm heading home."

Hass shrugged. "It would have been nice to bring Aballo in, but the money's the real prize. William was over the moon when he got your telegraph. The train people never expected to recover half the amount. You've made the company look good."

Capilano said, "Too bad about Rucker drowning like that. You ever work with him before?"

"Once," Oliver said, "a long time ago." Apparently Carmen and Marietta had dumped Rucker/Waterman's body into the lake. It had been picked up by a fisherman and brought into the harbor a few hours after Oliver regained consciousness. He learned of it after he'd walked into town, changed clothes and headed for the village barbershop. The story circulating there was that Waterman had passed out from drink and fallen off the cliff on the edge of his property. Nobody suspected foul play and nobody seemed to care.

Ignoring Capilano's questioning stare, Oliver turned to Hass. "Before I turn the loot over I'll want a receipt from William and my share of the reward."

"That's what we're here for," Hass said.

Two hours later Oliver boarded an end car and found a seat to himself. After the train pulled out he took a sheet of paper out of his vest pocket. It had been left for him at his hotel in Put In Bay. He unfolded the letter and re-read it.

Dear Ollie, now you know I wasn't deceiving you. You haven't been poisoned. I wouldn't poison the father of my only child. Really, by persuading you to sleep through the night Carmen and I have done you a favor.

You didn't really want to drag Hermione's young man off to jail. Ruining his life would have weighed on your conscience. Now you won't have to worry about that. By the time you get this letter the lovebirds will be safe in Canada starting a new life together.

Let's hope they make a better job of it than we did. At least they have a chance—more than we ever did. But we aren't done with each other yet, are we Ollie? I'll be seeing you and Chloe. Soon. Until then, all my love, Marietta.

Oliver refolded the letter and put it back into his pocket. He stared out the window at the Ohio countryside flowing past. It looked arid in the burning summer heat. Who would guess that a lake full of hard water was so close to these flat fields of grain and dried up grass? He thought about Baltimore. The water was hard there, too. But in quite a different fashion. He leaned his head back and closed his eyes.

# # #

Dear Reader, if you enjoyed this book please post a review. Independent readers depend on reviews to find readers. Thanks in advance, Louise

The next Oliver Redcastle, ***Trouble in Tampa***, is a Florida Writers Association Silver Palm Award winnder.

Here's a few of the opening pages:

1885: twenty miles from Tampa on the last leg of Henry Plant's newly constructed Jacksonville, Tampa & Key West railway.

The train screeched to a halt. Passengers thumped to the floor. A woman screamed as she tumbled off a bench, and her feathered hat slid down over her nose. Oliver Redcastle had been watching two boys toss apples at a gator on the riverbank. Caught off guard by the sudden stop, he jammed his shoulder into the back of the bench in front of him. Nursing his arm, and wondering whether he'd broken a bone, he pulled himself to his feet. Two men cradling shotguns crashed through the door into the car and stationed themselves at the head of the aisle.

"Settle down, folks. This ain't a robbery. We're lookin' for an escaped criminal. Be quiet, and we won't trouble you."

They were both in shirtsleeves and suspenders, their faces flushed and sweaty. The speaker, a short man with a wiry build, wore a broad felt hat pulled low over his forehead. His cohort, a muscular six-footer, stalked down the walkway. At intervals he steadied his gun on his forearm and stopped to look closely into the faces of passengers still scrambling for their benches.

He halted to stare at Oliver. Of a similar height and physique, the two men stood eye to eye. The intruder's pale blue gaze drilled into Oliver's steady gray one. "Why ain't you sitting down like you were told, Mister?"

"What's this about?"

"Sure as hell ain't about you, Yankee. So mind your business."

Before Oliver could get another word out, a hand came down hard onto his injured shoulder. As it dragged him back into his seat, he turned to find a stranger's face inches from his. The man's narrowed brown eyes sparked a warning.

A commotion burst out at the other end of the car. Both armed intruders galloped down the aisle. A woman screamed, and a male voice yelled for help. "I'm Innocent! Kidnapped!" The stranger pressing Oliver to his seat leaned closer. He hissed, "If you value your life stay put, and keep your mouth shut."

"What's going on?"

"Nothing worth getting your head blown off for."

The sounds of struggle at the back end of the car grew louder and more violent. Oliver tried to look, but the stranger tightened his hold. Oliver struck out and yanked himself free. When he got up and turned, he glimpsed a pair of sockless white ankles. They disappeared as the armed intruders dragged a man's kicking body off the train.

Oliver started toward the doors when once again the stranger slammed him into his seat. Furious, he confronted the man.

"Lay a hand on me again and I'll break it!"

"Is that so? Well now, is that any way to talk to a Good Samaritan?"

"Meaning what?"

"Only an ignorant fool Yankee wouldn't know. Railroad men rounding up work gang escapees ain't polite. Interfere with them, and they'll shoot you dead. You being a meddling northerner, they'd enjoy pulling the trigger."

Like a sleepy dragon jolting to life, the train began to creep forward. Oliver shot a rueful glance toward the back of the car. He judged it already too late to do anything about what had occurred. Nor was he sure that he should. After all, William Walters hadn't sent him to the south to interfere with local law enforcement—if that's what he had seen.

The other passengers seemed to have no trouble putting the incident from their minds. A motherly woman in charge of three youngsters opened a picnic basket. Behind her an elderly gentleman adjusted his neck cloth as he carried on an animated conversation with his plump wife.

Oliver rubbed his sore arm and turned to the man who was now bending to rescue his crumpled hat from the floor.

"I still don't understand what happened."

The man rested the hat on his round belly with one hand and steadied himself on the swaying train with the other. "All I can tell you is that the fella' those two deputies drug away was either a convict or a debt peon."

"Debt peon?"

"Mister, you're in the south. Around these parts folks who don't pay their bills wind up on a work gang. How do you think Henry Plant put the railroad through this jungle? Not by throwing a tea party for the local darkies."

"The man who just got dragged away wasn't a negro."

"No, that's why I say he was a debtor, or a foreigner who answered the wrong call for employment. Either way, there's nothing you or I can do for him."

Oliver regarded the speaker. His gray handlebar moustache framed his small mouth. His fringe of gray hair brushed a sweat stained collar. He inclined his head. "Wendell C. Hartley at your service."

"Oliver Redcastle."

"Pleased to meet you, Redcastle. Guess I riled you just now. Believe you me, it was for your own good!"

"If you say so."

"Well, I do say so. I know what I'm talking about. You didn't even realize I was sitting behind, did you? Before this ruckus started you was a million miles away staring out the window."

Oliver shrugged. That was true.

Hartley nodded. "I been in the cab up front. It got so infernal hot I thought I'd see if I could catch a breeze back here. I'd just set myself down when those two fellas stopped the train."

They were both silent, eyeing each other. Hartley broke the awkwardness. "Going to Tampa on business or pleasure?"

"A little of both." That wasn't true. Oliver didn't expect to get any pleasure from this trip.

"Me, strictly business. I don't travel otherwise. Travel don't suit my constitution the way it did when I was young." He winked. "I sure detect from your accent you ain't from anywhere near here."

"Baltimore."

"Baltimore?" Hartley's eyebrows jumped up. "Now what kind of business would bring a Baltimore man to Tampa? Bet it has something to do with this new railroad of Plant's."

"Maybe."

Hartley chuckled. "Half the people on this train wouldn't be in Florida otherwise. Thanks to Henry Plant northerners can escape from snow and ice in comfort."

"If you call this comfort," Oliver said, raising his voice over the clack of the rails, "and if northerners want to come to Tampa."

"You ever been there?"

"Never."

"Thought not. Well it ain't much now. From what I hear, Plant reckons to turn what used to be a sleepy fishing village into paradise on earth. He even plans to build a grand hotel the likes of which will stun even a sophisticated fella' like yourself. Tampa's going to become a regular seventh heaven."

"How heavenly is it now? I'm going to be spending several days there."

Hartley shrugged. "Any place where it don't snow ought to be paradise for a northerner this time of year. As for myself, I don't plan to linger."

"But Tampa is the end of the line."

"For Henry Plant's train, not for me. Now, if you don't mind, I think I'll head back to the front car. It's no cooler here than it was up there. In fact, I'd say it's hot as hell back here."

Louise Titchener

Visit my web page at
http://www.histrymysteries.com

Made in United States
North Haven, CT
28 September 2022